THE APPRENTICE
STRONG WOMEN

TESS MOLESWORTH

Published by Tess Molesworth

tessmolesworth@gmail.com

First published 2025

Text © Tess Molesworth 2025

The moral right of Tess Molesworth to be identified as the author of this work has been asserted.

All rights reserved.

Without limiting the rights under copyright reserved above, no part of this publication may be reproduced, stored in or introduced into a retrieval system, or transmitted, in any form or by any means, without the prior written permission of both the copyright owner and the publisher of this book.

For any copyright queries, please email Tess Molesworth at tessmolesworth@gmail.com

This is a work of fiction. Names, characters, places, and incidents are either the product of the author's imagination or are used fictitiously, and any resemblance to actual persons, living or dead, business establishments, events or locales is entirely coincidental.

 A catalogue record for this book is available from the National Library of Australia.

ISBN 9781763584624 (Print)

ISBN 9781763584631 (eBook)

Publishing support by Debut Books

Editorial by Stephanie Cuthbert

Cover Art & Formatting by DAZED Designs

Printed by IngramSpark

FOREWORD

Hello readers,

This is just a quick note to let you know what this book has for you and if you are ready to dive in.
This book was written in British/Australian English and may have some mistakes. You are more than welcome to contact me at: tessmolesworth@gmail.com with your concerns or praises for this story.
The main male character, Flynn, has a traumatic past (domestic violence, teen suicide of a family member). If these are a trigger for you, please take care of yourself. There is a HEA, so don't worry, he finds his 'forever'.

Happy reading,
Tess xxoo.

*Dedicated to everyone who has found their people,
person, friends, lovers. Cherish all the memories.
Don't give up. When you have a belief, a want, a dream,
a desire, let time lead you. Soak up the moments, cherish
the minutes, love the hours and value the days.*

CHAPTER 1
KATE

You've got to be fucking kidding me.

The blaring alarm on my phone wakes me, screeching loud enough to raise the dead. I swear I only went to sleep twenty minutes ago. Looking at my phone, it's actually three hours, but that's not enough. That doesn't even count. I was sure tonight my dark-eyed, dream beau was coming back for a visit, to wander through my sleeping mind, fixing all my issues.

Realising that it's not my actual alarm, but the security system going off at my new build, my mind finally understands there's danger. Fuck. Could this whole situation just end already? It's the third time this has happened this month.

At least this new system has me knowing there could be destruction happening before too much irreparable damage is done. At the work site there will be an alarm going off with all the intensity that the next county over could hear it. It's a new subdivision, so there aren't any neighbours. At least that's one less thing to worry about.

Grabbing my keys after throwing on a hoodie and tracksuit, I'm hoping when I get there it'll be an easy fix. Attempting to beat the sheriff to the site gives my two in the morning brain a kickstart to get moving. It's always good to have something over Sheriff John. Nothing like good banter between community members.

Pulling out of my drive and heading to the build, I wonder who else would be out on a night like this. There's not an inch of light other than the full expanse of stars.

Once I reach the edge of the city limits, I can see the strobe light of the alarm going off at the build. I sigh as I see the flash of the sheriff's lights mix with the white light from the security system. Shit! I shake my head. I'm sure once this little issue is dealt with he'll happily hand me a smartass comment or two. But for now, I know it'll be professional. That's the good thing about this community, the sheriff actually gives a shit and wants to make sure everything in his community is safe from sunup to sundown and all the other hours. He only ever recruits the best deputies to uphold his standards.

Parking my truck, I see the deputy has what looks to be a young man in handcuffs on the ground at the front door of the colonial house. The deputy, Colin, is standing next to the suspect. I give him a quick nod and search for the sheriff.

The security system I bought from EvaTech can only be shut off by myself or someone who has the code. Pushing a few buttons and answering the security questions: *where'd your mother go to school?* Hum, Croatia. *How many siblings does your father have?* Twenty-three. The alarm and the lights go dead in an instant. Of course, both answers are wrong, considering they grew up here, but a hacker doesn't know that. It was even tested on some tech buddies of my brother Logan from EvaTech. It took them too long. They couldn't crack it and they're the best in the country. Of course, Logan had no idea how my brain worked to get the answers, and he couldn't help his buddies either. You have to answer the two questions correctly and in a timely manner. That was a good party. Normally I don't go out with Logan, but I'd had a rough time with the builds and the vandalism, and I tagged along. I probably shouldn't have hooked up with Mac. He was a good laugh, a great fuck and after I'd been stirring the little genius about not being able to crack my codes, I thought I better pay him back for trying. I didn't know he'd be the one paying me. Whoever taught that man how to fuck, I need to thank them. He even managed to teach me a few things and it's my body.

Seeing John walking through the house with his

flashlight, I catch up with him. "Hi John, it doesn't look as though there's any damage. Anything I should know?"

"Just the busted lock on the garage door. Found the suspect huddled in the corner of the garage with his hands over his ears, practically rocking in fear."

Normally we don't find anyone when we get to the sites. This has similarities to all the other incidents that we've had, still, something different is stirring in my stomach.

"Are you not telling me something?" It just wasn't adding up. This was the first time the new system had been activated, but still my gut was telling me something more serious was going on.

"Deputy Colin found tyre tracks leading away out back, like before. But the suspect was in the garage. He hasn't said a word. Yet. He's probably waiting for the ringing to stop in his ears from that damn siren attached to the alarm system."

I smile, knowing this is exactly why I'd got the system. Glancing around with my own flashlight, everything looks to be in place. Previously, we'd come across paint splashed up walls and the ceiling hanging in various sheets. Whoever is doing this knows their way around a building site and what can make the costliest amount of damage.

"Alright, let's go see what we can get from him." I run my hand down my face in exasperation. I'm not an expert at questioning people, I just need to know what this man is doing at my build.

Making our way back to the front of the house, I realise I've got another lock for the garage door in the truck that I'll have to fit and replace before I leave. This night is too similar to the others. My sites are getting hit when there's no natural light and no neighbours, or no way of evidence being tracked back to them. It's why the sheriff and I had discussed the alarm system.

Stopping with the sheriff in front of the suspect, he kicks him in the boot to get him to look up at us and that's when my breath catches in my throat. A lump forms so quickly that I can't even swallow. I'm frozen to the spot.

Looking up at me are the darkest eyes ever put on this earth. I've seen those eyes for as many nights as I can remember. They've been in my dreams. They've chased my demons away and they've captured my heart. Because sitting on the steps of a partial build is that most handsome man I've seen and I can't tear my eyes away.

CHAPTER 2
FLYNN

How was I supposed to know this house was alarmed? I'd snuck in while they were packing up, watching the truck pull out and away from the building site. I just needed to rest. I'd been on the run long enough for all my rations to be gone and sweat to cling to my whole body by the time the boss lady had left. I'd watched the site from just over the ridge waiting to make my move.

I could see the building crew packing up and getting ready to leave at the front of the house, so I slowly made my way to the garage. Not wanting to draw attention to my approach, I managed to slip into the garage undetected and was able to curl up in the corner where I fell instantly asleep. I was beyond exhausted. My body had been pushed to its limits needing to escape my past. However, there was no one who could withstand the screech of the alarm system that woke me from my dead, exhausted sleep. Before I knew it, I was handcuffed and sitting on the front step of the house with my ears ringing to the point that I don't know if I'll ever hear again.

I've kept my head lowered because I'm still so exhausted and the ringing is not letting up. I just want to sleep. I have no idea where my backpack is. It's probably still in the garage where they found me rocking from the alarm. Not that there's anything that personal in there, but it's all I have.

The kick that comes to my boots is both unexpected and awakening. I flinch and raise my head. The deputy is standing there, only he's been joined by two other people. My exhaustion was trying to take me back to dream land, although the ringing in my ears is not giving up. The sheriff is now standing next to his deputy. He's obviously returned from his inspection of the house after putting me in handcuffs.

The light from their flashlights isn't shining directly in my eyes, but the sight of the third person has me wishing I could rub my eyes to ensure I'm actually awake and looking at who must be the boss lady. Looking pass them, I recognise the truck from earlier today. Everything about her is screaming power and I know it the moment her eyes meet mine. Even in the lack of light the flashlights are casting around the otherwise pitch-black night, I know her eyes are crystal blue, like the clearest day in summer.

I can see the sheriff's lips moving, but my head is full of static, and my ears are still ringing from the damn alarm. I've never wanted to hear more in my life. Though she's no longer looking at me, I witnessed the quick intake of her breath when her eyes meet mine. I see the sharp rise in her chest. If only my damn hearing would return. I could inform them I had nothing to do with the alarm going off. At least I *think* I had nothing to do with it. I don't even want to attempt to speak without hearing her reply. I doubt I could even hear myself anyway.

The sheriff reaches down and grabs me under the arms, yanking me to my feet. I've never felt like a tall person, even though I reach close to six-foot-two at my full height, but when you've been pushed down and made to feel small, you rarely know your personal worth. Standing close to the boss lady, I tower over her by nearly a foot and yet she makes me feel small. There's something about her power and stance at this site that has me wondering just where else she'd be powerful.

The sheriff walks me toward the patrol car, and I brush pass, lightly touching her shoulder. The electricity is instant. The quick pick up in my heart has my legs stumbling as my whole body wants nothing more than to be near her. My arm is covered in goosebumps, and I've never felt like this before. The sheriff places a hand on my head and guides me into the back. I nearly have to fold myself in half to fit in the backseat.

A small whisper of sound breaks through the ringing, and I hear murmurs of his conversation with the boss lady. I manage to grab her name. Kate. Then the door is shut on me. Not that I ever had a chance with her. However, the electricity in that slight touch is still coursing through my system, and the feeling doesn't lie.

Kate.

Simple. Elegant. Strong. Independent. Warrior. The determination in her stance as I look out the window at the most remarkable woman I've ever seen in my life, has my heart racing, pushing my blood to every extreme in my body.

The patrol car moves off toward the station for lock up. My ears are still ringing and for the first time since this all happened, I'm repeating her name—Kate—instead of worrying about me.

Back at the station, the sheriff's lips are moving again, but I can't hear a damn thing. Only patches of words or sounds are getting through. I just keep shaking my head, hoping that he understands I mean "I can't hear you", not that I'm disagreeing with what he's saying. Seeing the frustration on his face, he turns and scribbles something on a piece of paper. Turning back, I read:

Can you not hear because of the alarm?

I nod. This is progress. At least he's reasonable enough to not just throw the book at me. He turns back to write another note. I sort of feel sorry for him that this is how he will have to communicate with me for the time being.

I'm going to put you in the holding cell. We'll talk tomorrow.

Nodding again, I wait for him to grab me and take me to a bed for the night. I stand there, not being able to hear anything, before I feel the sheriff remove the handcuffs and finally, I get to rub my wrists. I turn and watch as he closes the cell door. Making my way over to the bed, I groan, sitting down and feeling the softness at the small mattress on the metal bed. How could a mattress in a police holding cell be such a comfort? Except when you've escaped my history, this is paradise. Curling up I face away from the door, closing my eyes. Kate is the last thing on my mind and my lips as I fall into total darkness and sleep carries me further away from my past.

A noise wakes me. It's the sound of the cell door opening. Thank fuck, I can hear. There is no point in hiding, whoever is here to take me where I need to go, they've seen me flinch from being woken.

"It seems you've got your hearing back." The accent from the sheriff doesn't match his appearance. He's a broad shouldered man—as tall as me, and all muscle. For someone probably double my age he's certainly kept himself in good health and physical condition. His voice, however, is the quiet, gentle kind that swims around you, comforting right through to your soul.

"Yes, sir. Thank you."

He places a plate of toast and juice next to me on the bed and steps back. I have no reason to believe there is something wrong with the meal, but I can't just gulp everything down. I need to look as though I am in fact human and not an animal looking at his last meal.

Biting and chewing all the toast before washing it down with the juice, it's over too soon. I know it hasn't even touched the sides with the hunger pains I was facing yesterday before I found the building site, but at least it's something in my stomach.

The sheriff is standing just inside the cell watching me with high intensity. I'm used to the stare that he's giving me. The same look of all figures of authority and officials.

I'm starting to shake, worrying I haven't really escaped. It's just a different chapter of the same story. I lower my head and just sit there waiting for any punishment or consequence coming my way. What I didn't expect is to have the man walk further in and sit next to me on the bed.

"The evidence suggests you didn't activate that alarm system, but I had to follow protocol. Kate Trembley is one of the best people I know and she's having a hard time with vandals at the moment."

I keep my head low, and my facial features schooled so the sheriff doesn't see my reaction to hearing her full name. *Kate Trembley*. The woman with the crystal eyes. The strength of an ox and the beauty of a goddess.

The sheriff continues his speech running his hands through his hair, breathing deep. "I didn't think it was a good idea, but Kate is out in the reception area wanting to talk to you. I haven't run your prints or ID yet. I was waiting to see how you woke up this morning. That bloody alarm system she has put in her builds is warranted, but a headache."

Smiling at the pun, we rise, and I move to put my hands behind my back for the handcuffs. "I don't think you'll need those. Just don't make me regret giving you the benefit of the doubt."

Nodding, I move in step behind him and follow through the hallway, down to the waiting room. My body is reacting to the sound coming from the front office area. My blood is starting to tingle through my system. Giving me zaps of life with every step I make towards her. Her back is toward me when the sheriff and I step up and slowly she turns to face me. She's wearing a cap, with all her hair pulled through the back into a plait that hangs between her shoulder blades. It matches her small frame. She's toned in all the right places and every other place has curves that would have men lining up around the block wanting to touch every inch of her. Her frame may be small, yet her strength feels like she towers over my lanky frame.

Stepping up to me, she barely reaches my chest. Her power and authority is different. It's something that had to be earned from hard days and long nights. Except her crystal blue eyes are fighting to reveal the protection she's yearning for. I failed to protect people in my past, but this feels like a test I'd pass with flying colours. It became second nature to stand in front of harm for those who need it. And something is hinting that Kate Trembley needs protecting.

I could just fold in on top of her and protect her. The sudden instinct to ensure she's protected has me more aware of my surroundings and where we are. This looks safe, no other man here to hurt her. The sheriff has a wedding ring on, I know he's no threat to her. The elderly lady behind the desk has life-lines written all over her face and looks as though she's been here longer than the furniture.

Stretching out her hand toward me, she says, "I'm Kate Trembley, owner of Make-It-Able Construction, which is the building company's house you were sleeping in last night. I have a few questions for you, before I decide what the sheriff should do."

I hold her gaze, though my mind is quickly coming up with a variety of scenarios to ensure I keep this woman safe and not lose her after the first question. No one needs to know the hell I've come from. These people have been more comforting to me than anyone has since my mother died seven years ago.

Grasping her hand in a shake I reply, "I'm Flynn Davies. Pleased to meet you". We're both nodding at each other like a couple of bobble heads on a dashboard.

"Let's take this outside. I'm a little uncomfortable in the station. Sheriff, we'll stay within sight in case I need you. I don't think Flynn here will give me any trouble, though."

Kate leads the way out of the station to a bench positioned in the front area surrounded with thick luscious grass. This allows me some personal time with Kate and if for no other reason, I'm thankful it's here and not with witnesses.

She sits at one end of the bench, and I move to the other. Not because I want to be away from her. It's so I don't scare her and draw attention for the sheriff to come out and lock me away forever.

Fidgeting with her hands, she folds them in her lap and looks up to my dark eyes. In the past they've been the things that have brought me so much pain. It's the memory they hold of my mother that led to more pain than any child or person regardless of age needs to experience. But I hold her stare. Her crystal blue eyes are darting all over my face trying to find some place to rest peacefully, that aren't my eyes. I think she's found a place on my cheek. I'm not sure why she can't look at my lips, I know I'm looking at hers. I'm sure my hearing is fully returned, however I don't want to miss anything that comes from her mouth. It seems Kate has a purpose to being here and the longing in her eyes is captivating.

"Flynn," she breathes my name out like it has been caught in her throat. "Like I said, I have questions."

Nodding, I've learnt when it's best to speak or silently acknowledge when to wait.

Kate continues after scanning my face again for a better spot to focus on. "How did you get into my building without the alarm going off, and why were you there?"

Lowering my head, I try to think of a reply that is not a lie, but not a whole truth. Plus, her eyes pierce me right to my soul. Her captivating blue eyes the colour of a bright summer sky, shoot tingles through every fibre in my body. I can only hold her gaze for a short amount of time.

"I snuck into the garage before you had left and curled into the corner and passed out from exhaustion." At least that part is true. Now for the trickier answer. "I'd been travelling for some time on foot and public transport when I could. I came upon the subdivision towards the end of the day. I didn't go into any other part of the house. Just the garage."

I look down into my lap and wait for the response Kate will give to my answers. It was all true, but will it be enough to satisfy her interrogation?

"The sheriff wants me to press charges for breaking and entering." I snap my head up to attempt to get a read on her decision. The look in her eyes seems guarded. It's like she knew that if I looked in her eyes, she'd give me her secrets freely. "But I don't think you had any intention of doing more than you did. Plus, I believe you had nothing to do with the history of vandalism at my builds."

The last part comes out as a whisper, like she's ashamed something like this has happened to her. My instinct is edging to come to the surface and protect this woman. I may not have the best track record protecting people I love, however, it doesn't stop the guilt crawling over my skin and through my pores to my inner demons living below my skin.

"So, what are you going to do?" I sheepishly ask.

Kate is keeping her head down. She holds all the power and there's no way I want to challenge or influence her decision by looking into the crystal pools of her eyes. "Flynn look at me." I raise my head as she continues. "You're to come and work with me as a form of community service. It'll be off the record, but it's the easiest and safest result. Your backpack was retrieved from the building site and the sheriff has it. Please don't make me regret this decision. I'll wait here while you go get it. Hurry up though, we're already late."

I nod because there's not much more I can do. I'm too dumbstruck by her generosity to give me a chance and not throw the book at me.

"You won't regret it," I say as I smile down at her from my height. Our eyes have conversations our brains and mouth can't comprehend.

Racing into the sheriff's station, I ask the receptionist about my backpack when the sheriff walks out of his office with it. "She's a good woman Mr Davies. I will be checking in on you every now and again. I don't trust you, but I respect her, which is why I'm allowing this to occur. If you so much as cause her hairs to stand on end, I'll have you thrown in the state penitentiary quicker than you can say your full name. Are we clear?"

"Yes sir," I reply politely, because he really does seem genuine. Little does he know that I'll never do anything to cause pain to Kate Trembley.

I grab my backpack and make my way back out to the bench, but Kate isn't there. Fear has me stopped in my tracks searching for her, I'm finally able to move again when I see her leaning on the hood of her truck. She's on her phone with her back to me. Taking in all her workers curves, I have to tell my cock to calm the fuck down. I've never had the urge before to take any action with anyone. I know other eighteen-year-olds have a different person every night. It's been suppressed in my life so that the feeling never became more than a passing thought back in high school. But seeing the curve of her ass highlighted in those tight work jeans, I know I'll need to tread very carefully around my new boss. Sleeping with her is not the answer to the demons of my past or the uncertainty of my future.

CHAPTER 3
KATE

My foreman Rick Jones calls me as I watch Flynn go into the Sheriff's station, and the timing is impeccable. I need the distraction from the long, lean limbs of Flynn's retreating body. I hadn't gotten any sleep last night once I'd fixed the lock on the garage and returned home. My bedding looked like I'd crumpled everything up and tossed it around the room to have it all land on the bed again. In the end, I got up and did a workout down in the basement gym. Every time I closed my eyes Flynn's dark orbs were staring up at me.

"Why the fuck didn't you tell me about the alarm?" Rick demands down the phone in his way of greeting once I answer the call

A little confronted at his tone and demand, I get defensive. "Firstly, I'm the boss, which means I don't need to tell you anything. Besides, you're not working on that site."

Rick seems to recover quickly from my response and is telling me about the stages of the other building sites. It seems the new build at the Belmont Estate, which is the only one with the alarm system, was the only one hit last night. Previously when one building site had been hit, others had been damaged in the same night. Rick has been with me for five years, and in addition to that, I've known him since my apprenticeship days. He was with me in the beginning of Make-It-Able construction when I left my previous partner and employer, Noah Fox.

"All other sites are still on schedule and all workers are back on deck this morning. What is happening with the suspect from last night at the Belmont Estate?"

I'm not sure how he got the information about the suspect, but I ignore that little mind niggle and focus on what he actually needs to know. He may not directly judge me, nevertheless, he has always found subtle ways to add snide remarks, until I remind him where his next pay cheque is coming from. There's something about Flynn that I need to look into, and it's not just his eyes. "He's coming to work with me today and I'll decide from there."

The silence on the other end of the phone is deafening. It's not only the cogs I can hear turning, but his filter is also working through his mind as well. I am the owner. I know what is best for *my* company. I don't need a man to tell me how to run it. I am here to make it in this world.

"As long as you know what you're doing." Which I know is code for: 'If this goes wrong, I'll be the first to say I told you so.'

"Thanks Rick. Flynn is coming. I'll talk to you later."

I hang up before he says anything more. I don't care what he thinks. It's my company. Fuck, it's a partial anagram of my name and I'll run it how I want. If he wasn't so good at his job I'd fire him on the spot. Anyone can be replaced.

"Is that all you have, Flynn?" I've seen bigger backpacks on school kids. "Actually, how old are you?"

Looking more sheepish than I've ever seen a man, he whispers his reply while kicking in the dirt and looking at his feet. "It's everything I have. And I'm eighteen."

Letting out a little breath, not wanting to show any sort of weakness, I'm relieved that at thirty-two I'm not employing a minor without consent.

"Alright. Let's get going. We'll stop off at the workwear shop to get you some clothes." His head snaps up and eyes bore into mine. I know he's going to protest. I stare him down and hold up my hand. "It's not safe to work in that gear and you'll pay me back when you can. I won't have an employee of mine not in the correct safety gear."

I finish and walk around to the driver's side. There's just something about him that makes me want to stand my ground and protect him. Maybe even want him. Fuck. I can't think like that. I'm the boss here and I need to remember that.

He's definitely not Mac. That man was too confident, but Flynn has an air about him that has me feeling like I need to protect him. Help him. Guide him. Whatever it is, he's not like any other apprentice I've come across.

My town is a reasonable size, constantly growing with people wanting a change from the big city, and I know I have just enough time to talk before getting to the workwear shop in the industrial area. I may as well make a start at getting to know this young man, because he's the mystery I want to solve.

"Flynn, how will you be able to help me at the building site you were at last night? Do you have any skills?"

Granted I probably should've asked him these questions while we were on the bench in front of the police station, but I wanted him away from the watchful eye of the sheriff John. He doesn't approve of what I'm doing. I suppose no one will. But that's nothing new in my life. No one gave me a chance to make it in the building industry. I'm proving them wrong every single day.

I can see the trepidation on his face as he sorts through what information he's prepared to give me. If there's one thing I know I can do it's read people. Even the mysterious man of Flynn Davies is no different.

Finally, he answers. "I did wood and metal work at school and finished at the top of my class in both. I'm good with my hands and can think quickly on my feet." He pauses for a moment, and I quickly glance over at him knowing he's got more to say. It's written all over his face and the fidgeting of his fingers is a dead giveaway.

"I'm sorry about your build and that I couldn't help you more with who tried to break in last night. I was too exhausted to move, otherwise it would have actually been me that set off the sensitivity of the alarm."

He really doesn't have anything to apologise for. Yes, he was trespassing, but in comparison to other incidents from my builds, he's done nothing wrong.

Giving a small smile, I can feel his eyes on me. The skin under my shirt is prickling with his gaze. Thankfully it stops at my sleeves, and he can't see the goosebumps covering my chest.

"Thank you." That's all I seem to be able to say. We drive the rest of the way in comfortable silence.

After getting Flynn kitted out in the correct gear for a builder in the trade, plus a few extra sets, we arrive at the building site in Belmont Estate. There's a skeleton crew working on the interior walls downstairs.

This allows me the time to teach Flynn the basics he'll need to assist me to hang the plaster in the few rooms upstairs that need doing. I don't normally work on the tools much these days. It's why I started my own business—so I could get others to do the work for me. However, I need to teach Flynn.

In the tray of my truck, I get out all the tools we'll need. The plaster for the walls is already stacked in the foyer. I know I can lift the sheets up the stairs, but I think I'll enjoy the view of Flynn carrying the sheets up there. I lift the first lot and show him the easiest way to manoeuvre them and try my hardest not to swoon at the sight of his muscles at work.

Fuck, what's wrong with me?

I shouldn't be thinking about how his muscles are working and holding the sheet of plaster being carried up the stairs. As we're walking back and forth between the piles of plaster, I can't help but notice the ease that he has doing this form of manual labour. He told me that he was a fast learner, I just didn't think a young person would be so focused on such a tedious task. Shaking my head from staring, I need to remember I'm the boss. Fuck, I'm fourteen years older and the bloody owner. Thinking about this young man as anything other than a worker is not how I wanted to start my day.

Once there are enough sheets of plaster we can start to hang them. I call Flynn over and demonstrate how I was taught to hang a sheet of plaster. He watches intently, taking in all the instructions and I need to focus on what I'm doing so that I can leave him to do it. Being this close to him is playing with all my emotions. His dark eyes continue to bore into me. I know it's because he needs to focus on how to do this, but I feel like his eyes are reading everything in my soul.

Stepping back, I watch as he follows the instructions I'd given him. He hangs it exactly how I did. If any other person had come up here, you wouldn't be able to tell the difference between the two sheets. They stand side-by-side like pillars. Looking at his work, I feel comfortable leaving him to it. I'll be working in the other rooms on this level. I leave him to it and the instruction to come and find me if he has any questions.

The morning flies by with us working, moving from room to room on the second floor. It's like we're meant for each other. *Now that's a thought.* What the fuck? Those thoughts can just fuck right off.

Watching Flynn, I can see he takes care to finish the job quickly and expertly. It's hard to believe that this is his first job. His appearance says he's a worker, although his quiet demeanour is one that suggests there's more to his story that he's hiding behind the walls he's erected.

I need to stay on schedule with this build—just as much as I need with my other builds. I never thought I'd need the extra hand. Flynn is proving himself to have the skills to make a great apprentice. A great employee, to be honest. Stopping briefly for lunch, then getting straight back into it, we work through the haze of the day. Dancing around each other with sheets of plaster, it's mid-afternoon by the time the second floor is completely sheeted.

Packing up and heading downstairs, we quickly join the crew and finish the whole house. What normally would've taken all day and some of the next, now has us all standing around looking at more of a house than the bare bone wooden planks that were on display this morning.

"I think this calls for a drink. You guys coming to the pub?"

A chorus of yes, ma'am comes from the other guys who were working on the plastering today.

They laugh, knowing I hate being called ma'am, and we pack up all the gear. I do a quick walk through to make sure the house will be ready for painting tomorrow.

Knowing Flynn is the only one within earshot I ask, "You alright coming to the pub with us? You've certainly earned it today with what you've done. I doubt we'd have achieved what we did today without your hands on the tools."

He seems hesitant. I'm not sure why he won't take the compliment. "Please Flynn, come with us to the pub. You can meet some of the other crew members."

His eyes are as wide as saucers as I add this last part. Shit, does that not appeal to him? Finally, he puts the tools in the truck and relaxes a fraction. "Ok, I'll come."

He's shuffling his feet like he has more to say. I just stand there waiting for him to form the sentences. It's easy to see them swirl around behind his eyes.

"Kate." He pauses again. It's cute watching him trying to make order of his thoughts. "Please keep a tab of everything I owe you. I won't be a charity case to anyone. I promise to pay you back. I'm underage, I don't know if I'm allowed in the bar?"

Looking up into his dark, obsidian eyes, I can see the truth in this declaration. At the ripe young age of eighteen, fourteen years younger than me, I know his soul holds the truth. He's worried about money and debts.

Reaching, I place my hand on his wrist. "I know Flynn. I know. It'll be ok. They know me and my company."

Standing there touching him, it seems life stands still. His eyes are holding me captive. I know I need to break away. These are the eyes that have always been in my thoughts, in my dreams. Having them in the flesh has every nerve ending in my body firing to the point of pleasurable pain.

Breaking the trance, I start by removing my hand from his wrist and then lowering my eyes and finally breathing. I didn't realise how shallow I'd started breathing.

Making our way from the tray of the truck, I watch

as he walks like there is something weighing him down. That's easy enough to pick up on. But there are times when he seems to live in the moment, maybe even a future and his presence is something of ease. As he gets closer to the passenger door the ease of life comes into him.

Hopping in, we peel out, making our way back toward town and the pub. It's a comfortable silence in the cab. The low hum of the radio means sound is filling in the spaces that we're not ready to accommodate.

"Kate." His voice shakes me out of my head, ensuring that I'm listening to everything he has to say. It's a gentle voice, one that holds information, emotion and himself. "It's too soon to tell you anything truly personal. But what I will say is, I'll never bring trouble to your door, and I'll be forever grateful for all you've done for me."

His gaze is straight ahead with his hands fidgeting and twisting in his lap. After the experience of touching him before, I don't want to do that while I'm driving. I want to reach out and calm his hands, but I don't trust my body's reaction. I don't want to have an accident. I want to take his troubles away and bring him comfort. But fuck, I'm his boss. I'm fourteen years older and less than twenty-four hours ago he was found in my building site trespassing. These feelings need to take a hike. My first priority should be figuring out the vandalism, not having feelings for Flynn, my apprentice.

Looking at his profile, his emotions aren't written there. It's like only his eyes hold all the keys to who he is and the secrets behind his wall he's built for protection. Whatever has happened to this gentle soul, he has to hide it away. Without looking in his eyes you'd swear he'd have the best poker face. One that could clean out Vegas.

Knowing we haven't far to go I need to quickly add, "Flynn, the guys may be a little hesitant toward you. We've had quite a few incidents over the last six months or so. They may not take to you straight away. I've found as the newbie, or minority, stand your ground and humour always works best."

I watch him nod his head in acknowledgement. His features change just a little, like his preparing to wear another mask.

Pulling up, most of the other crews are here. At least this is the best way for them to meet Flynn. By now word would've spread to all the men about Flynn and how he came to work with me. But I'm the boss and I'll take on anyone I want, and I'll let go anyone who threatens to take down my company.

Fuck, now I need to school my features otherwise some of these fellows will know something's up. A few have been with me since the beginning and they wouldn't cross me, but they'd cause enough banter for me to threaten their wage.

Locking the truck out of habit, rather than necessity, I watch Flynn make his way to the front of the truck. An easy smile is waiting for me and I know it's another mask. It's in his eyes. Not truly knowing the real Flynn Davies, his masks are becoming easier to recognise.

CHAPTER 4
FLYNN

My nerves have been rolling like thunder clouds leading a storm since Kate asked me to drinks at the pub.

I'd managed to get through our time together because I knew how important these projects are to her, and I can't let her down. She's taken a chance on me. She didn't have to. She could've let the sheriff do whatever he wanted, but those crystal blue eyes hold something.

When she looks into my eyes it's like she's searching my soul. Yet while she's doing that, I'm doing it to her. I want to know everything about his woman. Her strength has to come from somewhere. Her beauty is soul deep, well beyond the exterior curves.

While sitting here in her truck, thoughts flash around my mind. What can I tell her after less than a day of being with her, that won't have her running to the hills or kicking me out? She's even protecting me against her crew members. If she knew what I've survived, she'd know that her protection wasn't needed, but it wouldn't go unappreciated.

The hardest scars to heal are the ones you can't see. And they're the ones that I can't share with her. I have a few scars across my back that have never seen the light of day, so I know they're safe from her.

Making our way to the front door of the pub, I step up and hold the door open for her. That initial hit of 'pub' smell is always the worst. At eighteen I haven't spent a lot of time in an establishment like this, but when you know it, the smell will always hit every memory button on its journey through your senses. The memories I have, they're not the fun, happy ones. They're ones that leave scars and freeze limbs.

Gesturing for Kate to go ahead of me, it's not just so I can look at her beautiful curves— it's gentlemanly. I have no idea what I'm doing here. This is the closest I've been with any female who wasn't my family, and my first job or workplace function. This is unknown territory for me.

I notice Kate is a little shy, but recovers quickly, so fast that I may have just thought there was a sparkle in her eyes at the gesture of me holding a door open for her. I'm glad she hasn't discovered just what I'd do for her. After a short time, I don't even know the extent I'd go for her. All I know is keeping her happy is number one on my list.

I follow her closely, just not too close that it looks like I'm her shadow or a lost puppy. Her work crews probably think I'm a charity case as it is.

Stepping up to the tables, Kate announces, "Guys, this is Flynn. He's working with me for a bit. He's my new apprentice."

Thank fuck my past has taught me how to keep control of my facial features, including my eyes and stance. Apprentice! Fuck! I thought I was just here for the community service, not a fucking full-time job and trade. This woman is truly more than she gives herself credit for. I'm completely shocked and thankful with what she sees in me.

I wave at them, nodding in recognition of their presence. A shy "hey guys" is about all I can muster at this moment. I want to get a feel for the members of her team. I'll wait to start my banter and fit in more. Their eyes are registering a few different emotions; anger, betrayal, curiosity, weariness. They don't trust me and that's fair enough. I know why I'm here and I know how I got here. And the only person I have to impress is Kate.

Kate nods at them and starts to move towards the end of the table a little away from the main group of workers in various trade attires. She leaves enough chairs between us that we may be able to have some privacy.

"Can I get you a drink?" She raises an eyebrow with a little quirk on her lips. "Don't worry Kate, I can afford this." I'm not sure if they'll even serve me, but it's the least I can do for her at this stage.

Recovering quickly and pulling her face back into a neutral position, she says, "This is my shout, there's a tab. You don't have to pay for anything. It's just no one ever offers to buy me a drink."

Well, that's one up for me. I now know if I treat this woman as more than just my boss when it counts, she may realise I'm not leaving anytime soon.

I stand there waiting for her drinks order. Shaking her head with a smile, she says, "Thanks I'll have a spiritless. Just tell them you're with us and get yourself whatever you want."

Walking off to the bar I feel heightened that I'm able to do this little thing for her, especially after all the small things she's done for me.

Waiting at the bar, an empty beer glass is placed next to me at the same time a slap lands on my shoulder. Looking towards the man who violated my space, I see a man about my height. Tradie muscles covering his legs and arms proving he's been in the industry for some time. A collection of colourful paint splatters covers his attire and body. He hadn't been sitting at the table when I was introduced to the group. Clearly, he had been here somewhere else. I notice the 'Make-It-Able Construction' insignia over his left pec.

"Rick," he says, extending his hand. "I'm the

foreman. I was talking to Kate about you while you were at the station."

His introduction is contradictory. I can hear his smug authority at being the foreman and yet his gesture is a warm one. Although I feel there's more to this guy than the first meeting.

"Flynn," I say, taking his hand and not flinching at being touched. "I didn't see you at the building site today."

Turning, I see the barmaid standing there. "Sorry. May I please have a spiritless and a coke thanks."

Rick puts his order in as well. He turns back to me, "No I was at another site. Surely you didn't think Make-It-Able only had one job going? I was across town working and coordinating another job. Kate normally does a bit more around the sites and administration jobs, but she's taken you on, so I've had to step up today and for a while I suppose now that you're our new apprentice."

His condescending tone is not lost on me and this guy is sending up all sorts of hidden negative vibes. He obviously doesn't want anyone to read him. My past also taught me to read people and their vibes. I think I'll be keeping a watchful eye on this one.

"How'd you find your first day?" His question doesn't take me by surprise. It's the fact that he'd all but belittled me with his introduction and now wants information. Two can play at that game.

"I've found a few different muscles, but it's nothing

I can't handle. All the plaster and sheetrock has been hung in the house at Belmont. I guess it's ready for you and the painters now."

His shock is easily spotted on his face. Clearly the other members of Make-It-Able hadn't told him how much we'd accomplished today.

"Perhaps we'll make a worker out of you and not some freeloader."

I smile while I grab the two drinks and turn to make my way back to Kate. "Next step is your job."

He doesn't know how serious I am about that comment. I think I've just found my other reason to stick around. I want that slimy bastard's job. His tone and attitude is enough to have me looking out for Kate and her company. He may be a foreman, but she's the boss. And boss trumps foreman every day of the week.

"You and Rick seemed to be getting along at the bar. He's a good foreman. He's been with me since before I started Make-It-Able."

Taking a refreshing sip of our drinks gives me time to think about my reply and not to blurt out what I'm thinking. "He was surprised when I told him everything we'd completed today."

"Trust me Flynn, when I walked back in the house this morning I didn't know if we'd have all those walls finished. I honestly couldn't have done it without you. Are you sure your dad wasn't a tradie? You certainly know your way around a building site and nail gun."

"I told you I was a fast learner."

"The cuts in that last room were a nightmare, but you managed to put it all together."

"I figure if you take your time and focus on the main parts it all just falls into place." Maybe that last comment was a little cocky, but it wouldn't hurt for Kate to know my ability and confidence. "So, what are we doing tomorrow boss?"

The light-hearted approach and jest in my tone has her trying to hide her emotions. In less than twenty-four hours I'm getting better at reading her. Plus, when she looks in my eyes, I can read so much more. Her crystal blue pools are loving the sound of 'boss' coming from my lips and her eyes shine more brightly.

"The painters normally come in next, but they're all busy on other builds. This one can't wait until they're ready, so I guess I'll be teaching you how to paint."

The mirth on her lips is reaching her eyes. If her teaching me to paint is as successful as hanging plaster, I'm going to love every paint covering minute.

"You know I can handle mess. Let's make it messy."

I smile while what I said slowly sinks in. Hiding my smile behind my glass I take a sip. I didn't even know this side of me was in there, but this woman knows how to bring out all my sides. I can see the cogs in her brain trying to come up with a reply.

"Who's getting messy?"

Not showing I've been overheard a little, a man sits

down on the chair next to me. I guess I'll have to speak even more quietly for the next innuendo. Looking around, Kate has recovered enough to show the relief at not having to reply. "My name is Drew." He extends his hand in a welcoming gesture, before turning back to Kate. "Sorry Kate, the Reiss place hit a few snags, and I wanted it finished before I came out."

"Flynn," I say, acknowledging his introduction. "How's it going?"

If I'm sticking around, I may as well seem civil and not just focus on Kate. This guy seems friendly enough.

"Same shit different day, joys of a plumbing life."

"Yeah, I hung around all day. Joys of a plasterer's life."

Throwing his head back and laughing, Drew reaches out for his drink. "Yeah, Kate he can stay. I like this one."

Who'd have thought that my bad joke would be a hit. His easy way of approaching everyone and making them feel comfortable has me thinking I could call Drew again for another after work drink.

Platters come out and are placed along the table. Drew and his jokes get worse as the afternoon drags into twilight.

As tradies begin to get up and leave, I acknowledge the ones that make an effort to recognise me as they say goodbye to Kate and respectfully thank her for the drinks and platters.

Drew starts to rise. "Flynn, it's been great chatting and drinking with you. See you on a site. Thanks Kate. I've got to get back to Brad before he tans my hide more than I want him to." He winks at us as he finishes the rest of his beer and walks out.

There's only Rick and two others at the furthest end of the table. Talking softly, I know they won't hear our conversation.

"Kate, sorry to ask, but do you have somewhere for me to stay tonight?" I've reverted to my shy, reserved demeanour. It's an uncomfortable situation. She's already done so much for me that I shouldn't be asking for more, but I don't have any other options. I hope that she hadn't set something up with Rick or the other fellows that are with him. They don't look like the type of men who'd want a house guest for an undisclosed amount of time.

"Yeah, about that, I have a spare room. You can stay with me."

I need to see her eyes. They won't focus on me, looking just past my face. I can't read her.

"Thank you." What else can I say? It's a shy reply. The appreciation can be heard though.

Finishing off our drinks with small chats about what we need to do tomorrow at the site, we make our way to Rick and his buddies. "Rick, the tab is closing off. I'll see you around. You all good at Hillview tomorrow? We'll start painting at Belmont until you can get there."

Kate holds a professional tone as she lets him know her plans. It seems she is aware of how much he can drink. And yet she continues to have him working for her as the foreman.

Just as she's about to turn and leave, Rick pipes up. "Where's Flynn staying tonight?"

"That's none of your business. I've got it covered."

"You know I worry about you, Katie."

The slight cringe in her body tells me that she doesn't like it when he calls her that. She recovers too fast for the others to register her movements.

"I know you do. Thanks Rick. Night."

She's turning and making her way to the bar to close the tab and take care of it all. Rick's eyes narrow as he watches Kate leave toward the bar. I step into his line of sight to protect her and let him know that it's not going to slide with me. Noticing all the rum and whisky cans on the table these three have certainly consumed their fair share for a mid-week evening but I doubt they'll feel it tomorrow. I've lived through the signs of what an alcoholic can get away with.

"What you going to do, lackie?" He sneers.

Raising up to my full height, "Whatever it takes, drunk."

Turning, I make it to Kate in time to hear the total of the tab as she hands over her card. Her smile doesn't reach her eyes even the barmaid gives an apologetic look. Yeah, all of us know that it was Rick and his buddies who racked up the bill.

Placing my hand on the small of her back, I guide her out of the bar. At the truck I'd offer to drive, but I've no idea where we're going. She feels like her bones are weary in her skin. God all I want is to take care of her.

CHAPTER 5
KATE

I nearly forget Flynn is with me as I enter my house. The absence of the screen door hitting me while unlocking the front door is what drags me from my exhaustion and to the realisation Flynn is still with me and I'm not alone. For the first time in a long time, I'm glad to have someone with me.

Shit. He's been with me since the bar, and I can't remember if I've spoken or even acknowledged him.

"Sorry. I'm not a very gracious host. This is my house." Stumbling through the door, my words and everything seem to be blurring. "Of course this is my house. Shit. The tab at the bar, no sleep last night, working all day, I'm just exhausted."

Noticing his wince at my comment about last night, I cringe again.

Fuck, what's wrong with me? "No Flynn, it's not your fault about the alarm and all that." *Actually, it was your eyes which I can't look at now*. Those dark pools coming to life from my dreams continues to play havoc on all my nerves.

"Kate, it's ok."

He's looking around the house taking it all in and I'm too exhausted to care about the state of my house.

"I'll give you a quick tour."

I feel dead on my feet. I haven't felt this tired since I first started my company and learning to juggle all the tradesmen, the builds and my own workload.

I point out the ground level areas briefly: lounge, kitchen, laundry in the back. At the stairs which lead down to the basement, I explain there's a gym and entertainment room down there for when you need to escape the world above.

I find myself being held up by a solid wall of muscle. Flynn has stepped up behind me and with his hand resting on my hip, ensures I'm still able to function. How is he so attuned with all I need? It's like he can read everything I need. I didn't realise I needed an apprentice, yet from his help today, clearly, I could really use him in my crew. It feels comforting, reassuring and natural. I lean into him. It shouldn't be like this, but right now Flynn is all I want.

"I'll show you upstairs and where you'll be sleeping."

Leading the way up the stairs, I know Flynn is right there behind me. Already I feel he's got my back. All day he's proven himself to me. It seems ridiculous after less than a day these feelings are stirring. I don't even know his story. But I know he cares.

Standing in the middle of the upper level, most rooms can be seen from here. Pointing them out, I say, "That's my office. Next to that is your bathroom, with all the amenities, and clean towels are in the cupboard. Your bedroom is across the way. My room is at the end of this hallway. And that's another spare room."

The sound of running water pulls me from my monologue of the standing tour. Walking I see Flynn leaning into the large shower testing the temperature of the water. "Right well I see that you're getting comfortable. I'll leave you to it." I'm too exhausted to stay and it's not my place to watch this man shower.

Turning to leave, I'm stopped by a hand on my wrist. "No Kate, this is for you. Come here. I guess you have an ensuite up there, but I don't want to leave you alone right now. You said it yourself—you're exhausted. Let me look after you."

"But why?" I'm bone tired, swaying, but also loving the attention. I've known this man less than twenty-four hours and he's wanting to take care of me.

"I had to look after my mother when she got sick. I haven't had to care for anyone in a while and I know you need this. If I'm wrong, tell me to stop."

He's pulling my reluctant body towards the glorious warm spray covering the black marble tiles lining the shower.

Drawing me even closer he begins to undress me,

starting with my shirt. Lifting it up over my head, I should be worried about what he thinks about my body. But right now, the steam escaping into the overhead fan is all I focus on. I know if I look in his dark eyes, I truly will fall and there's no escaping the depths of those pools.

"Keep going." It's all I can muster from my lips.

His fingers continue to graze over my body as each layer of clothing is removed down to my comfortable workwear underwear. Watching as Flynn quickly removes his work shirt and leaves his singlet and work shorts on. He gently moves me into the shower.

The warm spray covers my body and starts to loosen my muscles and wash away all the problems of the world, until I'm standing there humming quietly to the feeling of strong hands caressing my back with a loofa and soap.

Being held steady by Flynn is adding to the comfort of the shower.

"Kate, I just want to take care of you. After all you've done for me in such a short time, it's the least I can do."

"What was your mum's illness, Flynn?" It may seem like a personal question in such a short time, but that felt like an opening. The shower gives me a little energy, restoring some human capabilities.

"My mother met her end from a mixture of spiritual and human influences. She'd endured enough in this world that her spirit gave up and her body didn't take long to follow."

Cupping his face, his dark eyes hide the pains of the past so well that I can't read his feelings. "Thank you for telling me that small part of you. Our past holds too much power unless we let it out." He leans more into my hand as we stand there with steam moving between us.

At the first tinge of cold coming from the high-pressure rain head, Flynn is turning off the shower, and wraps me up in a towel, lifting me up in his arms, carrying me bridal style toward my bedroom. "Do you always carry women to their bedroom the first time you meet them?" Making a joke to hide my exhaustion and comfort of being in his arms and relaxing us from that overwhelming revelation. For someone so young he has muscles and strength enough to carry me and all my curves.

"Only the ones that need me to. Do you think you'd want this treatment every night?"

His smirk is lighting a way through my body with more heat than the shower. Standing at the end of my bed, Flynn looks like he's a little unsure of what to do now. Reaching up, I kiss his cheek with hidden promises of more to come when I'm not as tired. He turns his obsidian eyes looking deeply in my crystal blue ones. It feels like our eyes are having the conversation our mouths are unable to. Lowering his mouth, he kisses me just as lightly on the lips, expelling a small moan from me in the process.

"Kate, I could kiss you all night and every hour of the day, but you need to rest and I want to get out of these wet clothes. Goodnight, baby. I'll see you in the morning. Thank you for letting me stay." That little word meant a lot. Though, did he realise he called me baby?

He lowers me to the bed, turns and leaves me slightly breathless on top of my covers still wrapped in a towel.

I fumble my way through my nightly routine and crawl under the covers, realising that his scent is lingering on my arm that was wrapped around his shoulders. My eyes are too heavy to stay open and I fall into a dreamless sleep, nestled into my arm allowing his scent to sweep over my body.

CHAPTER 6
FLYNN

There is nothing better than a good night's sleep, although it didn't happen last night. After putting Kate to bed and organising the house a little, there was no heavy sleeping, but I managed some rest. Now, as dawn breaks the evening's silence, I'm in the kitchen wondering what I'm allowed to have for breakfast and how I can help Kate more.

I had an uneasy feeling as I was doing the laundry last night, and it didn't leave until the early hours. Seeing Kate as worn out as she was, I had to help somehow.

"Morning. Are you ready for another day on the tools?" Her soft voice pulls me from memory lane and shocks me. I didn't hear her approach. Normally I would hear everything, right down to a breath. I've lived my life on the edge, not many can sneak up on me.

"I've never shied away from hard work and I'm not about to start now." Pausing to take in all her features, coming to rest back on her face, I add, "I washed your clothes last night, although I can see you've got another set. And I don't know your morning routine or coffee."

I've never been one for coffee, never allowed to have it. I'd just settled for juice and toast.

"That's fine. Sorry and thank you for last night. That shower was everything I didn't know I needed."

She starts moving around the kitchen and every line and curve of her body has mine electrifying. My dick shouldn't be able to pulse at this hour of the day with the lack of stimulation. The memory of last night in the shower and the sway of Kate in front of me is doing everything to my body. It's a double attack.

Every sense is focused on her. Attuned to her soul and the instant her eyes lock on mine, regardless of the length of time, it's like our souls are reaching out to each other. Pulling me toward her. Toward her soul. She's leaning by the sink, waiting for her morning tea to be ready. I reach around her, lightly touching her arm and place my dishes in the sink.

Her pulse is racing and without realising it her hands are on my hips holding me right where I am. Half covering her body with mine, inches from hers. Our breath is ragged, matching our racing hearts.

She rises on to her tiptoes. I lower my head, just enough to show I'm ready for anything she wants to give me and respect her choices. "If we start now, I know I won't stop." Her lips are lighter than a feather as they ghost over mine.

Lowering back to her natural height she giggles and slips from my reach, walking to the toaster to deal with her bagel.

My life is changing by the millisecond, and I know all I want is Kate Trembley and anything she'll give me. All I can do is smile and shake my head at the ease of it all. Less than two days together and already there are sparks and teasing.

It's not long until we're walking out to the truck. I notice a few crushed flowers that weren't there last night when we arrived, but it could be anything. I'm not going to burden Kate with something as trivial as that. I just file the thought away. Seeing her carefree, I keep the flower observation to myself.

On the way to the site, Kate is going over all our tasks for the day. "So, once I've got you all set up for the day with the painting, I'll need to go back to the office and just check a few things. You good with that?"

"Yep, whatever you need."

Pulling up to the work site, we make a start straight away. Kate goes through the motions of prepping and cutting-in. Watching her down on her knees, I can't help myself. "Are you going to be watching *me* while I'm on my knees? You look a little too comfortable down there."

Her eyes widen instantly, then blink and her surprise at my comment is gone. In its place is the boss.

"Focus. This isn't some joking task. I need you understanding all that I'm showing you."

Nodding as an apology and the international sign to continue demonstrating. She finishes showing me how to roll-on the undercoat.

I'm aware that with Rick being the head painter in her team, plus second in command, perfection is not good enough. It needs to be so professional a God couldn't fault it. From what I observed last night, he doesn't like me sitting on his turf.

After an hour or so of Kate's observations and tutelage, she leaves me with the radio and a bare house. The goal is to have the whole house done today, honestly it would be pushing it. I'll just put my head down and see what happens.

The hours are filled with repetitive labour and great music. I don't realise I'm hungry or how much I've achieved until Kate is standing in the lower office area holding hot food which is caressing the inside of my nostrils, and her profanity reaches my ears.

Turning toward her, the shock on her face couldn't be more evident. "Fuck. You're downstairs already?"

"That depends. How much have you seen?"

"I've been upstairs. I heard where the music was coming from and couldn't believe it. But after seeing upstairs I truly can."

Everything falls silent long enough for my stomach to grumble and she giggles at the remarkable timing of it all.

Putting everything down and going to wash up, we find a makeshift table and chairs for our dining room. The first bite has my mouth letting out a pleasurable moan that has my cheeks going the colour of a tomato.

"That noise isn't something I'm used to hearing on a job site, Dark Knight."

Dark Knight? What could she possibly mean by that? How could I be anyone's hero? My eyes were normally seen as the villain in a story because there is just one shade difference between the iris and the pupil. When you're told often enough that your soul must match your eyes, you rarely lift them to another person.

The hint and innuendo of her comment isn't lost on me. "It's not a sound I'm used to making, Boss."

Her eyebrows shoot straight toward her hair line. Every question about my comment is written on her face. The most glaring one... *'Are you a virgin?'*

I'm not answering that until I have to.

The meal is finished up with small talk, avoiding any thoughts of what my previous comment alluded to. I start to clear things away and get back to work, but Kate's reaction is quicker. She's standing over me holding her hand out for the rubbish.

Lifting it to her, she takes more of my hand than just the garbage. Holding everything with the power of her crystal blue eyes.

I'm in a trance. Sitting on the up-turned empty paint drum, I'm more than folded in half. Reaching only to her lower ribs, I have to strain my head back to look up at her. I'm not used to looking up at people, the joys of my height. Yet having her above me is something I could get used to.

Her eyes keep me captivated. She's standing between my outstretched legs. My other hand is on her waist. My thumb rubbing circles across her hip bone. The rubbish falling from our grasp and completely forgotten.

"Wh-what do you want?" Stammering because I've no idea what all this chemistry means between us. She's my boss and I'm nothing important to her.

"I'll stop if you want." Her voice is honourable. Her eyes hold no desire to stop. She wants this as much as I do. Her legs are moving ever so slightly against my thighs.

There is no way I can stop her. Whatever her plans. Her actions. I just hope I'm good enough for her.

She cups my face. Eyes penetrating all the way to my soul. Taking in all my emotions. It's a whisper I'm not even sure at the small distance she could hear me. "Don't stop."

The perfect timing of her lips descending to mine makes our first kiss feel like what legends are made of. Her hands hold and direct my face to the angle she wants. I am completely under her control and there's nowhere else I would want to be.

Her tongue pushes at my lips and without any

second thoughts I open to grant her access. She already has entry to my soul, why not my mouth and that's where the battle takes over. My tongue dives into her mouth. Together we dance around each other's tastes.

Her hands leave my face to coast down my body, looking for the feel of skin on skin. I take the action as an invitation for my hands to start their own exploration of her body.

As soon as our hands find flesh our bodies ignite with passion. The feeling of a fiery passion flows through my body and has every fibre tuned to Kate and everything she has to offer.

Standing up, I cradle her ass and lift, allowing her legs to lock around my lean hips. Walking over to the kitchen bench and laying her down, I kiss my way down her body and expose her flesh along my journey. Her breathing starts to pick up, giving me the encouragement to continue with my adventure.

The goose bumps covering her flesh are heightened from the light nips, sucks and kisses across her beautiful body.

I may be a virgin, yet everything I'm doing is pure animal instinct. I know all I'm doing can only be for Kate. Her body responds to every action with silent encouragement to keep going.

Undoing the button and zipper on her work pants, her breathy pants come harder and faster.

"Yes. More. Fuck, give me more."

Lowering her work shorts and underwear to her

ankles. She's slightly trapped because of her work boots and it's this restraint that has me aching to explore her beautiful curvaceous body more.

I saw her body last night in the shower, yet this view has me more eager to perform. Without a second glance, or second thought, I dive between her thighs and lick through her glistening lips.

The spasm of nerves is instant. The twitch of her legs traps my head at her apex and I know there's nowhere else I'd want to be.

With a combination of tongue and sucking, I work her clit to the point of climax.

Her moans echo around the open planned living space and I've never been so glad to have no neighbours in my life with the noises I'm pulling from her body. Her orgasm comes fast and the spasm of her inner muscles on my tongue leave me moaning on her wet pussy lips.

I could spend the rest of my life buried between her legs. Kissing my way back up her body, I coax her breath to return to a normal pattern. Licking the side of her neck, right up to her ear, I breathe, "I knew you'd like watching me on my knees." Hearing her giggle I add, "you okay?"

The erratic beat of her pulse can be felt under my tongue as she struggles to answer. "Fuck. I've never felt better."

Taking the compliment, but not giving up, "Oh baby, you will."

My smirk is covered with her lips, and she moans again. I know she can taste herself and it's the best fucking aphrodisiac as she tries to lick her taste from my tongue.

Moving her mouth from mine and kissing her way down my neck. "Do you want to get out of here?"

I can't resist the taunt that leaves my mouth. "It's the second day on the job. The boss needs this house finished. I have to stay and get it done."

My fingers slip into her wet pussy with ease and give a quick pump. The aftermath from her orgasm is covering my fingers and coating the kitchen bench.

Using my thumb on her clit, I coax her hips to rise and her back to arch, I can't help but watch all her features as I work her up again. This is giving me so much pleasure watching her respond to my every touch.

Sucking her neck, feeling her pulse below my lips is sending all my blood to my cock and it's all for Kate. I don't care if I come in my pants. It'll be embarrassing, but for her, I'll do anything.

Feeling how close she is, I pull my fingers from her and begin to walk away sucking her juices off my fingers wanting every taste I can get.

"Fuck the boss," she pants, sitting up on her elbows, watching me head towards the office where I was working before lunch.

I can feel her tracking my every movement. Her moans and frustrated noises are filling every space and following me into all corners of the house. I can't look back at her. If I do, I'll run right back and bury my head between her thighs. It's the hardest thing I've ever had to do. Walk away from a sexually high Kate Trembley.

Hearing her slide off the bench and reaching down to retrieve her clothes, I pause, knowing there's enough distance between us and turn to her. Watching as she rearranges herself, knowing she's still highly sensitive and wet, my reply reaches her faster than she can react. "Oh, I plan to, baby." And walk to the office.

CHAPTER 7
KATE

Why didn't we have sex?

God, Flynn Davies— my Dark Knight— is everything my body craves.

Yesterday we'd finished off prepping and undercoating the house at Belmont Estate. I had more to do at the office, but I was not leaving my apprentice. There'd been light touches, feather kisses and every time his lips were within breathing distance all I could smell was my scent. He'd savoured my essence.

The aftershock from the orgasm was felt throughout my body. The seam of my work pants would rub across my clit, or my damp underwear would send a fresh wave of moisture to my sensitive area. Along with the memory reel that started all these feelings.

The flirting had started innocently, and even on the way home he'd never crossed the boundary. I didn't want to push him. There was a reason he kept it light and innocent. Even though the feast my pussy gave him was anything but innocent.

Our evening was filled with light stories of our pasts, our loves, our families, but I felt he was holding back, like he was protecting me. The pinnacle was our shared shower. Flynn said he wanted to save water. I think he just wanted an excuse to be in my naked presence and he's the only man I haven't been self-conscious with in more than a decade. He doesn't see my workers curves or callused hands as a threat. More as an achievement to hard work.

Noah Fox, my ex-partner and the man whose only good quality was him introducing me to the love of the building trade, was a topic I danced around. I didn't want to dig up those memories and cast a shadow over our evening.

Noah and I had been together since the beginning of my apprenticeship. He was a lot of my firsts, including a broken heart. But like most innocent and insecure women, I stayed with him through the years until it was just too much.

I could've asked Flynn about the scars across his back. However, we weren't ready to dive into dark depths. I'd lightly touched one during our shower and his reaction was all I needed to know. His scars were his past to share in his time. Swimming in the light was where our evening had to stay. I didn't want to share my darkness any more than I wanted to hear his at this stage. That was for another time.

Flynn was different from other men from my past. Mac doesn't count. He was a playful, drunken fling, who knew how to do things and how to make you feel juvenile and young at heart. Noah Fox, my ex who I thought was the love of my life—the man who popped my cherry and taught me the building trade—broke my heart with words and actions. Neither of them compared to the gentle, caring soul of Flynn Davies.

Snuggling into Flynn's side, I told him if he wanted to continue working for Make-It-Able construction he had to sleep in my bed; naked. I had to give him a little push. I didn't want him to leave, it felt right for me. It feels right for my company and in the past two days, he's proven that. He's worked harder and more diligently than any other apprentice I've ever worked with. And this is my company. So, if anyone has an issue with my bed partner, they can be replaced.

Wrapping me in his arms and allowing a chuckle to ripple through every pane of his lean body, he told me. "There's nowhere else I'd want to be. But I won't have sex with you." That little comment had sent caution straight to my heart. I didn't know why he didn't want sex. I knew I just had to take whatever I could. Nuzzling into my hair he continued, "Not until I know that you're all mine and no one can tear us apart."

I started to wriggle from his protective embrace and

kissed my way down his body. Nipping at the smooth sections of his torso. Pleasurable sounds left his open, panting lips. I kissed my way from one hip to the other and avoided his pulsating cock. The twitching from the sensations of my mouth and tongue drawn from his body had a smile lighting up my whole life. He's so sensitive and responsive. Finally taking him in my mouth, his moan of pleasure filled every corner of my room. This room had never heard such sounds. I didn't stop my administrations of desire until I could feel every ounce of his cum sliding down my throat. Swallowing a promise of my own: Flynn Davies means something more than a fling to me. And that's the scary thought.

Now, dawn colours play across my wall. I hate the thought of leaving the comfort and haven of this moment. This bed. This man. But my company needs me.

Raising my head from his chest, I watch Flynn fight the smirk and leave his eyes closed. "Whatever you're thinking about, just stop. I can feel all your thoughts, even the ones you don't want me to know."

His eyes lazily open to reveal the obsidian colour that has my core clenching. Feather touches circle and swirl over my back, and I can't help but squirm into his body.

"Are we getting up to start the day?" he asks.

My hand travels over his abs and rests around his cock. The slightest touch has it growing more than just morning wood. It doesn't feel right gripping such smooth and virginal skin with my callused, overworked tradie hands, but there's no better way to wake him fully up. His response gives me the encouragement to move my hand from base to tip.

He sucks in a breath. "Jesus, baby. It's taking all my restraint to not take you here and now." His panting breath has me wanting to break. I want him. "I can't Kate. I want a forever with you. And I know that's ridiculous after only two days, but please stop. I won't take advantage of you."

Why can't I get my fill of this man? Fuck, what is wrong with me? I'm fourteen years older and we've brought each other pleasure, but I can't commit? I'm his boss. And his scars tell me there's more than enough trauma in his past that I need to back the fuck up. Let's not forget the insecurities that Noah planted on my soul, which have grown a few roots over the years.

Get it together Kate. Act your age.

The inner voice telling me he is only eighteen seems to be getting louder the more time I spend with him. Plus, I'm his boss. He is my apprentice. This is not what I wanted when I started my own company.

Removing my hand, I lightly kiss his chest before getting out of bed. Flynn falls back asleep while I'm getting ready. Seeing him at such peace, I decide to leave him there snuggled in my bed. Writing a note and leaving it on the bedside table with a phone I bought for him, I head off to work.

The high of having Flynn in my life, both personal and professional is a comfort I never thought I needed. I've always done everything on my own. Once Noah showed me his true colours and I came to my senses, I realised I didn't need anyone. I could do it myself.

The short distance to the Belmont Estate is nearly broken by the need to turn around and be with Flynn. But the euphoric feeling of Flynn slowly starts to dwindle. Something has happened. It just feels wrong. The closer to the building site I get, my gut starts to flip. From the outside everything looks normal. On closer inspection I nearly collapsed from pure exhaustion and defeat. The questions rattle through my mind and numb my whole body.

How did this happen with my new security system? Why did they hit it again so soon? Who would do this? Why are they doing this to me?

Gathering all my strength, I leave my truck and move to inspect the damage.

Whole walls have been torn down, everything but the load bearing pillars. SLUT. WHORE. HARLOT have been spray painted on various surfaces. Stairs have been removed. Whoever has done this knows the building trade. They knew what would cause the most damage with the highest excess insurance payment.

The rubbish and debris from the attack needs to be dealt with and the sheriff needs to be called, but the fact that the security system didn't work last night has me ringing the one man I didn't think I'd be calling.

After three rings he answers in a voice thick with cockiness and a sexy surprise only he could pull off at this hour of the day. Well, I'm about to rip his cockiness a new one. I'm struggling to contain my emotions.

"This is a pleasant surprise, Miss Kate. It's a bit early for a hookup."

"Cut the crap, Mac, what the fuck happened at my build last night?"

"Ok this doesn't sound good." All the cockiness leaves so fast you never know it was there and is replaced with concern. "What happened?"

"No shit, Mac. I'm fucked. Some asshole has all but demolished my latest build. Two nights ago, the alarm went off when the garage door was kicked in. And last night when I've had every wall kissed by a sledgehammer there wasn't a fucking sound. Mac, I'm done. This'll break me."

Hanging my head in my hands, I'm so lost. I don't know what to do. The security system had cost me enough, even with a bit of a discount. The numbers flying through my mind at the cost of all the damage, not including wages, are consuming and weakening my soul. Tears are building behind my eyes and I'm struggling to hold them back.

The rhythmic tapping of Mac on the other end helps to centre me. His attitude changed as soon as he realised this isn't a friendly call and that I'm hurting. Knowing he's on my side, helps to start rebuilding myself to a functioning state.

"I'm looking at your logs. I'm not sure why you didn't ring Miles or Logan. They both work at the company and all. But it says the alarm wasn't set."

"I didn't ring Miles because we both know he'll be balls deep in Blair and Logan wouldn't answer as quickly as you. And I fucking set that alarm. Flynn watched me do it."

"Wait, who's Flynn?"

"That's none of your business. But he was with me all night and is still keeping my bed warm as we speak. So, I know he's got nothing to do with this. Look there has to be something more. Mac, please you're the best at what you do, help me."

The plea in my voice has to count for something.

"You don't have to plead or beg. Leave it with me. Of course I'll help you out. Have you called the sheriff? Call him, get a team of forensics over there. I've got you, darling. I'll call you back as soon as I've got something. Breathe. You won't fall, I'll catch you."

"Thank you." His reassurance is everything I need in a friend. We hang up to the sound of Mac tapping faster at the keys.

I call the sheriff, and it isn't long before the red and blue lights are lighting up the street. Sheriff John had told me not to touch anything and just looking at all the destruction, I couldn't stand inside for too long anyway.

I'm sitting on the front porch when the sheriff approaches. His intake of breath causes a wince through every muscle in my body. The destruction is that bad.

"Alright, Kate? We'll get all the evidence back to the lab right away and then I'll get some guys to come and help you clean up and get you back on track." Patting my back in a fatherly gesture, he adds, "we'll get them."

I will my phone to ring to take my mind from the scene behind me for a distraction. Maybe Flynn is ready for work. Although I doubt he'll want to come back to this site and see all the damage. The vibration nearly causes me to drop my lifeline. Seeing his name this morning is not the call I want. No time of day is right for him.

"Hello Noah."

"Katie, it's so good to hear your voice. How are you, gorgeous?" Hearing him call me Katie, has me nearly crawling out of my skin. I fucking hate it.

He never could read a situation. He didn't hear the pain in my voice. The strain in my life. Rubbing a hand over my head, calculating the timelines on how to attack the situation inside, I have to say, "Noah, now isn't the best time. What do you want?" Being short and to the point with him is the only way to get this over and done with.

"Well, I wanted to catch up with you and talk business. I hear you're doing brilliantly with all those new builds. Word is even reaching me all the way over here. After all I taught you everything, perhaps there's something you could teach me."

The silence stretches between us. I don't want to talk to this man, however he's right, I do owe him a lot. Perhaps I could meet up for a quick coffee. I also know Noah isn't great at hearing no. It wasn't a word that he'd heard a lot of, therefore doesn't understand the meaning.

I know I shouldn't meet with Noah Fox. His cheating arse shouldn't be within bull's roar of me, but he does know construction. And if I don't take some time to see him, he'll just come and interrupt my day more. Normally it's information about construction that he's after. Hopefully, he's finally given up on us getting back together.

I sigh down the line. "Meet me at the cafe in town in thirty minutes. I've just got to do a few things, then I can be there."

"Great, see you there. Oh, and Katie, come alone. No one needs to be part of our chats. It's just one business owner to another."

He hangs up before I could reply with why that even needed to be mentioned. Moving through to find Sheriff John, I explain what I'll be doing and where I'll be if he needs me.

"Something doesn't feel right. Be safe."

"Thanks John."

Patting him on the arm, I go out to my truck. I need to get Flynn more work clothes, then I'll go to the cafe to meet Noah. John was right, of course, something isn't right. My builds keep getting vandalised. Someone is out to get me, and I have no idea who it is.

Pulling into the work clothes shop, my phone rings again. I never get this many calls this early in the morning. Seeing Mac's name flash across the screen, I don't hesitate.

"Yes Mac."

"Oh darling, don't say that. It takes me back to our night."

This man, seriously! How can he make me smile when the whole world is looking at me laughing and pointing because I can't construct houses, and everything is falling down around me.

"This isn't the time for fun and games. Clearly, you've found something."

"Kate Trembley, you owe me. There's not a lot of people I would do this for. Your phone was hacked. That's how they gained access to the security system. They did a great job, but like you said, I'm the best. And they probably didn't count on you calling yours truly."

I take my first real deep breath. Finally some good news. I'd nearly abandoned all hope for the day and just drove back to Flynn so that I could start the day all over again in the hopes that it didn't happen.

"Who was it?"

"Vixen Dallas-Jones."

"What? Mac that doesn't make sense. Vixen has been dead for six years."

I could hear his fingers flying across the keys. Adding this bit of information to what he already knew. I can imagine him having all three screens lit up, with his eyes scanning the windows open seeing things that no other person would have a clue what it all means.

"Yes, I can see how you would think that. But everything I have in front of me about what happened at your building last night and with your phone, is pointing to Vixen Dallas-Jones."

"Look Mac, I've no idea what you're seeing and all that, but I was at her funeral. I went with Noah and Rick."

"Just be careful. I'll keep looking around and see what I can discover. You know me, I won't stop now that I've got a lead and I'm on the scent. I'm better than a bloodhound. Stay safe and stay close to your phone."

"Ok, thanks Mac. And yes, I do owe you."

We hang up again. The information just adds another layer to my already complex morning. At least I'm going to see Noah now and I can talk to him about it all. Although, he was completely heartbroken when his cousin, Vixen had died all those years ago. That was about the time Rick had started drinking. And why wouldn't he drink? Vixen was his wife. She'd died from an aneurysm and pregnant with their first child.

There are so many variables I've no idea where to

start. The vandalism. Noah calling. Rick's continued heavy drinking. Even Flynn's arrival. No wonder my brain is so flooded with information. I've nearly lost my bearings for why I started this company.

Noticing Noah's truck isn't in the parking lot at the cafe, I take another deep breath and get a look of myself in the visor mirror. Staring back at me is why I started Make-It-Able construction. To prove to everyone, I'm a strong woman who can take on anything... and win.

CHAPTER 8
FLYNN

Rolling over and burying my face in Kate's pillow is the best snooze button. Surrounding myself with her scent sends me to my comfort zone. This is where I'm supposed to be. Anywhere this woman is, is where I need to be.

The blazing sun dances across my body, letting me know I've clearly slept long enough. Still wrapped in Kate's pillow, I raise my head to look at the nightstand. The alarm clock says it's a little past the start of a working day. But it's the note and phone that quickly wipes the frown from my brow.

I scan the note and nothing but smiles and adoration cover my face, looking at her worker's script. Easy to read print with the added cursive letters and evenly spaced words.

I've programmed my number in. Call me when you need a pickup. xoxo.

Kisses and cuddles. This woman is too cute. I want to call it love, but is it too early? She's all I think about, and I honestly can't imagine a future without her.

Knowing I've left her without a worker long enough, I go about getting ready and send her a message.

FLYNN

> Sorry. I'm getting ready. Come and get me, please. You need me, xoxo

I had to throw in my own kisses and cuddles. There is nothing that can remove the smile highlighting my face or the butterflies of excitement in my stomach at being lucky enough to have found this woman.

Quickly having a shower and throwing my work clothes on for another hard and rewarding day, a knock at the front door startles me from the joy of going to work for Kate again.

In nothing more than my 'Make-It-Able' work clothes, I slip my new phone in my back pocket, and I open the door to see my past standing there and my heart plummets to hell. Past my feet and all the way to the demons below.

The calculating look on my father's face tells me my surprise is showing on my features and he knows he's won again. My mind is doing cartwheels with all the spinning questions flying through my head. After years of abuse, I know that I can't speak unless I've been asked a question or if he speaks. I never ask a question. Questions lead to cuts across the tongue. Small shallow, quick cuts. One for every word that was spoken without permission.

"You're coming with me." He moves his shirt away to reveal his favourite baton and I know there's no escaping. "It's you or the pretty girl I saw leave here this morning. Your choice?"

It's not a choice at all. There's no way I'd allow this monster anywhere near Kate. The fact that he even knows where she lives is enough to have me planning and processing every option to keep him far away from this town. Shit, even this state if I can help it.

No matter the cost, I will protect Kate. Even if that means I never see her again.

Stepping out with no boots or socks, I carefully close the door on my happiness and future. Following like a hollow man, because I left my soul on the threshold of Kate's house, I see the beat-up truck parked just down the street.

The beat-up truck that drove me to a hospital once out of the hundreds of times I needed to go. The beat-up truck that drove my mother out of my sight for the final time. The truck holds more secrets than a spy in any organisation.

With my head down and following my father like

an obedient dog, I start to put my walls back up, blocking out all feelings, all emotions.

Sitting in the front of the truck, ensuring the bricks are all in place, I don't see the swing of the baton landing on my thigh until it is too late and all that is left is the radiating pain I know from past experiences which isn't enough to break the strong bone.

God, I hadn't felt that pain in an age. He would rotate the torture, no real schedule as to when something would be happening. The memories of pain come flooding back, but it's the strength to not react that pushes through to the forefront.

I cringe because it's the only reaction I am allowed.

"At least you've remembered your reactions. The drive is going to be filled with little trips down memory lane."

"Yes, sir."

"I'm so glad that man, Noah Fox, rang me. I knew I couldn't put out a missing person's report. But it was only a matter of time before you made yourself known. After all those dark fucking eyes always led you to trouble. Just like your useless mother and twin."

There's no question in his ramblings and I've no idea who Noah Fox is. All I can do is act how I'm supposed to so Kate remains safe and away from harm.

That was the rule—he spoke, you acknowledged. No sound from him, no sound from me.

Another life lesson from Edward Davies, the veterinary assistant.

He knew how much trauma the body could take and how to bring it back. His study in blood drainage from a single hole, which wouldn't leave a big scar, was an unforgettable summer holiday session. Even the supplements needed to enhance healing so the time between beatings and torture sessions were amongst his researches.

The old beat-up truck rumbles to life as mine begins to fade. I was delusional to think I could beat this man. This monster.

For close to a decade, or at least the memories I have from my childhood, this man has ensured that if there was ever a happy moment, he'd beat two horrible memories into me to replace the happy ones.

Turning the truck around all I can do is begin the process to protect myself, to protect Kate. She is my everything. Even if I never see her again. I know she'll find happiness without me. Sitting in the front of his beat-up truck, I'm nothing but a body closing myself off to the world.

My memories of the last few days with Kate will be locked away until I'm away from this bastard. When I'm left to recover— whatever, my punishment will be — I'll relive all the beauty and happiness that my thirty-two-year-old boss was able to bring into my broken soul.

As we're halfway down the street with my future held up back at her beautiful home, a truck passes with a hint of recognition. But I haven't the time to think where I've seen it. The baton lands with precision on a spot an inch from the first blow. Edward Davies knows where to hit and just how hard. After all, he's had years of practice.

CHAPTER 9
KATE

Emotions are flowing hard and fast as I sit waiting for Noah in the café.

Noah and the mystery and timing of his call.

Mac and his compassion and determination to help.

The sheriff and his fatherly love and dedication to upholding the law.

And Flynn. Love. Caring. Empathy. Future. He just feels like everything to me. His ability to read my emotions and cater to my needs.

They're all swimming through my system trying to answer and analyse the feelings and emotions linked to every aspect of my life.

Having Flynn's body snuggled into mine last night and not having sex was another comfort I wasn't expecting. More than that though, I need to step back.

The vandalism is breaking me. I'm his boss and fourteen years older. I need to sort out my life. He doesn't need to be part of this mess. He's my apprentice, not my partner.

When this is over, I can have him.

That thought should scare me, not have me fighting a smile when worries cover my features.

Getting the urge to leave and fix my messy life, I face the window, and there's Noah's fancy Fox Construction truck pulling into the disabled park bay.

He's completely different to Flynn. Noah's arrogance surrounds him like a bubble. He spots me through the glass with his signature half smile, egotistical nod and I know it's too late to escape.

With his eyes only for me, he makes his way to the table in the centre of the room and places a kiss on my cheek like old times, before sitting down and not removing his hat. In our time apart it seems he still hasn't found any manners. He hasn't changed.

"Katie, it's been so long since we've chatted. I'm glad you came."

"Noah, I can't stay long. I'm a very busy woman." Getting to the point is the best approach to my arrogant past. I can't believe I agreed to this. If it wasn't for Mac's admission, I wouldn't be here.

I won't stay long, too many things need doing, and I doubt this man can help me. Besides, him calling me Katie really grates on my nerves.

"You look stressed and worried. Tell me how I can

help. I'm here to offer my workers, at a sub-contractor's rate or my services directly."

Wiggling his eyebrows suggestively, I know what that means. Is he serious? There is no way I'd go back to his bed. Surely, he only means with builds in general. He wouldn't know about the vandalism, right?

"Thank you for the offer, but I can handle everything. My crew are all on board and no matter what happens I know they've got my back."

"Are you sure about that?" His question has me wondering just how true my comment was. "Rick still talks to me, you know."

No, surely not Rick. He's been with me the longest. He gets the best jobs, wages, everything. Having to school my features, my curiosity is grating on my nerves. I want to know more. "I'd say he would still speak to you. He was once part of your family."

I can see in his eyes that I hit a nerve with that little comment. It seems that Noah still hasn't got over the loss of Vixen. I know Rick truly hasn't and that's why he drinks whenever the tab is open at the pub. What if Mac's discovery this morning is right? Could Noah be the person who is vandalising my builds?

"Rick may have hinted that you've got too many builds going at once and things are happening that you can't control. Katie, I just want to help."

I recognise this as his helpful, caring voice, but I also know it's not the true Noah Fox. That truth is burnt into my memory watching him fucking a woman in his work office.

"Rick also said you've got a new apprentice with no skills and a dodgy background working for you. That's not safe. I could give you a few workers."

Right now, the only thing that Noah Fox is giving me is a headache from bad memories. And how does he know that Flynn has a dodgy background? I don't know that much about his background.

"Rick shouldn't be discussing that side of the business with you. He hasn't even worked with my new apprentice." I will keep Flynn safe for as long as I can. "He is the hardest worker I've come across in my days on the tools."

Pride swells in my chest with the accomplishments Flynn has achieved in just two days. He's someone I'd trust with my company. I'm beginning to think Rick is no longer part of Make-It-Able construction.

Reaching into his inside coat pocket, I watch as Noah removes what looks to be a folded cheque and slides it across the table to me. "That's to help. Fuck, Katie. You're supposed to be with me. Come back to me." The violent whisper of his voice reaches across the table and tries to strangle my throat and worm its way back into my life.

Pleading and begging is not something Noah Fox does often. When he does it, there is violence and possession in his voice that would have lesser people shaking. I've been part of his life long enough to know the signs of his temper building. It took me a long time to realise what they were, now I can spot them as easily as faults in my builds.

The tune I programmed into my phone for anything to do with Flynn snaps my attention instantly. Reaching into my pocket quickly I read his message, and a smile caresses my face. Just those simple words have enough power to return the sunshine and chase away the clouds that come with Noah Fox.

"If that's about your new apprentice, it's bullshit. He won't stick around Katie. Not like me. I'll always be here for you."

Nearly giving myself whiplash for how quickly I move my eyes from the phone in my lap to him. My glowering stare is burning through to his blackened heart. "What do you mean?" My voice is as heated as my stare.

And there, staring back at me is the evil I remember. "Everything."

Leaning across the table with all the assertiveness of the boss I am, I whisper, "what the fuck is *everything*?" My voice is pitched low so no one in the café could hear. "Tell me what you know or so help me, I'll bury you and everything you love."

He must see the seriousness in my eyes because he leans back a little before the evil glint is returning to his eyes.

"I had someone do some digging and found his

past. Flynn Davies will never come back once he is gone." Leaning back across the table, I don't move away. Standing my ground, I can take anything he says to me. "And you'll be mine Katie. I'll own everything of yours, body, mind and builds. Flynn Davies is leaving without a trace," checking his watch, he says, "about now, I reckon."

I don't hear anything more. I can't leave quick enough. He goes to reach out to me, but I'm too fast. Pushing through the cafe, knocking over chairs and moving tables, I'm out the door before any sound has registered on my brain.

Fuck this can't be happening. Not now. I need Flynn with me. I need him to fix all this by my side. I need to know he's safe. And is Noah behind the vandalism? How about Rick? How deep does this go? Fuck!

Racing to my truck, I'm on the road back to my house in record time. I need my man. Yes. He's mine. *Mine.* No one else can have him.

My phone is ringing like wildfire, as soon as it finishes, it's going again. None of those tones are Flynn's so I'm not picking up. Turning down my street a feeling sits in my gut. It's like my soul already knows that its other half is missing.

My eyes catch a beat-up truck driving out past me and that's when I know. My brain has caught up to my soul. There in the front seat are the dark eyes of my life. My Dark Knight.

Pulling over onto my verge after nearly colliding with the beat-up truck, I'm out of my truck without turning it off and chasing the other vehicle down, screaming like my life depends on it. Neighbours peer out from behind curtains or open their front doors as I go to the end of my street and collapse to my knees. My throat is raw from all the screaming and yelling. Tears create tracks down my face.

Just as the truck is at the edge of my eyesight, I realise the plates belong to another state. It may take me the rest of my life, but I will find Flynn Davies. I will have a future with him. He will be mine. My forever.

Every cell in my body is on autopilot in the action to find Flynn and bring him back to me where he belongs. Back at my house, I begin the search for anything that could assist in my quest to bring him home. Right now, all I have are the truck plates.

Making my way back to the kitchen I realise he has his phone. That's all I need. Opening the app, there is certainly a benefit to having a brother in tech. My heart begins to slow as I watch the little dot flash and although it's moving away from me, it's a beacon to my soul.

Flynn had looked like a shell when he passed me. Whoever that man was held too much power over my apprentice. My man. The strong, caring, hard worker who had shared my bed was not the same man I saw in the front seat of the truck as it drove past.

Snapping from my minds torture of 'what ifs', I gather anything I'd need to get him back. I'll deal with them, and Noah—who I feel is behind all of this—once Flynn is safely back with me.

The dot tells me he isn't more than an hour in front of me and I'm not going to let him get any further away. Making it back to my truck, I'm on the road following my lifeline.

Continually checking the phone and GPS signal of Flynn's dot, the incoming call from Mac has me swerving, nearly causing an accident and waking me from my constant haze of thought.

"Why the fuck are you leaving town?"

His question comes through the Bluetooth speaker before I'd even fully had a chance to correct my swerving.

"Jesus, Mac. How do you know what I'm doing?"

"I know everything and more. Plus, I've hacked your phone to help you out, remember?" His voice still has the normal jovial approach, but there's a hidden anguish to it.

"What's wrong? Why do I feel this isn't a casual call?" Even though it couldn't be casual with what's happening. He normally makes a joke out of everything. The dot continues to flick at me, taunting me and reminding me why I'm leaving town.

"Normally I'd be every good thing you need, but darling it's not good."

Splitting my time between the dot on my screen

and the road, Mac tells me all about the vandalism and who was behind it.

"Are you serious? Mac this is bigger than just a little threat. What do you think we should do?" At least I know with Mac that when he holds secrets, he's the equivalent to Pandora's Box. This is a man who has more secrets stored in his head than all Heads of State in the world.

"First, tell me why you're leaving town. You need to call the sheriff."

"I'm going after Flynn. I just saw him leaving in a beat-up truck with a different state number plate."

"Makes sense. I'm not sure how I feel about my replacement. Just as well I've moved on several times since you. But you were one of the best. And still the only one I accept calls from." There's the jest that I've grown to love from Logan's gaming buddy. "I can ring the sheriff for you considering you're choosing to chase your heart."

With all the information Mac has dug up, there's enough to put everyone behind bars without seeing daylight for the remainder of their lives. However, this is something I need to take care of personally. I know he'll help me when I need it, but these bastards have messed with the wrong woman, and I am not beyond taking care of myself.

"I can't thank you enough. If I don't call you within the next twenty-four hours, send out the cavalry. We're not dealing with amateurs here. When I have your replacement back—as you so eloquently put it—those bastards are going down. Don't call the sheriff. Keep hacking if you need to and put the details together for me. Just wait until I'm back or you've heard from me."

"Darling, I've got eyes everywhere. Go and get your man."

There was nothing else to add to his comment. Hanging up, a new strength begins to form in my gut. It sends sparks all the way down to my toes and through to my soul. There is no limit to my determination to win this fight and get Flynn back.

It seems Noah had lined too many pockets and now he needs my business to continue the handouts and his lifestyle. His parents quietly cut him off when the first accusation came to hand. Mac had even managed to find the phone record that led to Flynn's father coming and getting my Dark Knight. Just another reason to take Noah down.

Adding to the information Mac had given me, I now know a little more history as to why Flynn didn't want to tell me about his past or those scars covering his back.

No one is a saint. There are black spots on everyone's soul. But people like Noah Fox and Edward Davies only have black souls. There is no light in their life.

The rest of the drive is focused on the task ahead. One thing at a time. Flynn is my first priority. I need him like I need my next breath, and I'll spend the rest of my life giving him everything I have. This man will only ever know love once he is back and in my arms.

Creeping past the address where my phone tells me Flynn's phone has stopped moving, I recognise the truck as the one which stole the love from my life.

Looking at the house, you wouldn't know evil lives in there. It looks just like all other houses on the street. Green lawns, flowers in the beds with no weeds. Clean fresh paint. Topped off with a porch swing. The sun is shining, illuminating everything at the address where Flynn could be suffering unfathomable horrors, if the lines of his past decorating his body are anything to go by.

Parking several houses away on the opposite side of the street, I feel the adrenaline coursing through my veins, and I have to act now before it burns out and I am no use to Flynn or anyone else. Reaching into the glove compartment I find my pistol and make my way over to the house.

Knocking on the screen, the house is silent on the other side. My stomach starts turning as I pray I'm not too late. Just because the truck is here, doesn't mean Flynn is.

Taking a deep breath, I bang on the door again. I don't call out. I have to maintain some form of secrecy. I want my presence to surprise Edward and not lead to Flynn's death as a convenience.

The sound of locks starting to move has me

stepping back a little and reaching into my coat pocket, resting a ready hand on the pistol.

The man has a confident presence, even removing the safety chain and opening the door fully revealing himself.

"What do you want?" His question is laced with annoyance at being interrupted. There is nothing to indicate what he's been doing.

Mac had given me a warning that Edward Davies seemed like a dangerous man, just through his dealing with Noah and other messages he'd seen on Edward's phone. Aside from the warning, the scars on Flynn's body weren't put there from surgeries or an accident-prone childhood. Trauma causes those marks to the flesh.

"I want Flynn."

There is no room for questions. I stand there staring this man down. He is nothing but the scum of the earth with no purpose. He towers above me, but I'm not backing down to this arsehole. He has what I want and I'm not leaving without Flynn.

Throwing his head back he roars with laughter. "You think you can come here and stop me. Flynn is my son. He's mine not yours. You're welcome to come in and say goodbye, but he will not be leaving with you... unless it's in a box. That's a guarantee."

That's my cue. All I need is a way into the house of horrors. Taking charge of my facial features and beating heart, I softened my features and hang my head in defeat. The act is award winning. "Fine. Lead the way. I want to see him one last time."

Gesturing for me to cross the threshold a shiver runs down my body as soon as I enter the house.

Waiting for Edward to relock the door, I follow him through the hall to the back and from somewhere in the back of my mind I see my opportunity. As he opens the door with a set of stairs leading down to the basement. I quickly remove the pistol from my pocket and smash it to the back of his head. Edward Davies falls, crumbling down the stairs better than any stuntman in a Hollywood blockbuster action film. With no time to analyse the situation, I follow him down. Pausing over his body I feel for a pulse and am rewarded with a light, slow beat, but alive. Raising my head with an intake of surprising breath, I find Flynn hanging from a butcher's hook by bound hands. He's in nothing more than his boxers, and other than a few bruises on his thighs, he seems unharmed.

I shudder a breath and run to wrap my arms around his hanging form. I'm not too late. Bruises are easier to fix and deal with than a body being drained from the butcher's hook.

CHAPTER 10
FLYNN

She came. If I didn't love her before there's no denying how much I love her now. Feeling her body wrapped around me, I'm briefly relieved of the pain from hanging off this butcher's hook.

"Is he dead?" I have to ask. I can't have her wanted for the murder of that monster.

"There's a pulse, but I don't want to be here when he wakes up. How do we get you down?" Her voice is muffled through deep breaths and having her face buried in my stomach.

The pain in my arms and shoulders has passed intolerable about halfway through being strung up here. "Over on the wall there's a lever that will release the pulley system and lower the hook and get me down," I say, indicating my head and she races over and sets the contraption in motion.

The release from being strung up like prize beef

always felt like heaven, but that was before I'd had this woman in my arms. My hands are still bound, my whole body struggling to hold itself up and all I can do is loop them over her head and hold her for dear life.

"Baby, are you nuts?" I mumble into her hair, not wanting to let go just in case. "You shouldn't be here. I did this so he wouldn't come after you. To protect you. And you raced down those stairs like a warrior? I've never loved anyone as much as I love you."

Kissing the top of her head and holding her body against mine is all the healing balm I need. I can feel my body putting itself back together because this woman came to rescue me.

"There was no way I wouldn't come. I watched you leave. My heart stopped at that moment. I would've been here sooner, but Noah Fox held me up."

Noah Fox. That name had been the cause of this whole thing. God knew how far back that bastard had created trouble. "He was the bastard that called my father. He'd paid him to come and get me. He told my father where I was."

At that point, more groaning came from the floor, making both of us stare at the lump there.

"Come on." I urge her to help make my legs move quickly. The bruises are causing pain and discomfort with each step, but I need to get away from the house of horrors that hold all my past.

Kate guides me toward the torture table and removed my bindings. Allowing the muscles and blood to begin to flow back to normal through my system. I waste no more time, capturing her face in my hands and cover her mouth with mine, giving her everything in a kiss. Every promise. Every love. Every future. It is all for her. She is all for me. Mine.

We stop at the top of the stairs to lock the basement door. It's a one-sided lock, I should know, I was locked down there more than once.

The worst was the night my twin, Miry took her own life. I was taking a beating, watching every swing as his baton re-coloured my skin. When Miry's soul had flown free, I'd felt the warmest, heartfelt, whole-body embrace and I smiled with the feeling of sorrow and strength she'd given me. He'd stopped mid-swing and couldn't continue that night, nor the next two weeks after. I was left alone down in the basement and only taken to Miry's service so my father could maintain his respected veterinary assistant status in the community. Then I was placed back in the basement, locked from the outside and only fed once a day or not at all.

On the main floor of my childhood home, it looks all warm and inviting, because people would come and see my father for out of hours veterinary needs. It's upstairs where the bedrooms are that the house looks unkept. There's nothing except my keepsake box I need from my bedroom.

Kneeling on my old bedroom floor, I pry open the floorboards and remove a small metal tin that contains all I'd ever want from here. I'd left in too much of a hurry last time. The moment the clock struck midnight on my eighteenth birthday I ran. My backpack had been packed and waiting.

Opening it up, there are a few photos and trinkets from my mother and twin. Kate is looking at its contents and her presence makes every heartache come to life. A single tear runs down my cheek. "I wish they could've met you. Or even found some peace in the pain that monster had put us through."

"Let's get out of here."

Nodding to give her the go ahead, we begin walking back through the house. Towards the front door, we increase our pace wanting nothing more than to be away from all the horrors this address has caused over the years.

"I'll give you a minute," Kate whispers and kisses my cheek, leaving me on my front grass, as she rushes over to her truck a little down the street.

Taking one last long breath, I'm standing at the end of my front path by the mailbox looking back at my childhood trauma, sending mixed prayers out to any deity that will listen.

The sound of a neighbour's screen door draws my eyes from the memories playing on reels across my mind's eye, while my dark eyes are searching the house hoping my father is still unconscious on the basement floor.

Mrs. Sommers comes and stands next to me, while

her husband waits on the porch watching us. I've lived next to these people my whole life. They were one of the first people to live in the street. "Flynn, we're sorry. We knew, but we didn't do anything. We all knew."

I turn and look into the sweet eyes of the elderly woman. "He's not dead." I don't know why I feel like I should tell her anything, but it seems right. There were small mercies from the elderly couple over the years and she deserves the truth. "Just unconscious in the basement."

Nodding in understanding the older lady gives my arm a pat and turns back to her husband, just as Kate pulls up to collect me and we leave everything behind.

Seeing this magnificent woman come to my rescue while not knowing the true danger she was in, makes me fall for her even harder than I thought possible. My heart had once been void of feelings, and I was barely alive. Now though, every breath will be making sure my woman is loved and cared for like no other.

I sleep most of the way back to Kate's place. Home. There's no other name for it. No matter where Kate is, that'll be my home. Walking into her ensuite, she follows me in. It all feels so natural, that she would be in here with me. With everything that we've been through since our first meeting... I never thought I'd be so excited and overjoyed to have been illegally found.

The warm water has healing powers, just not as much as Kate's gentle touches. Her caring hands work wonders on my bruises. Kissing along her shoulder and neck while she gently rubs away my past shouldn't be a sexual act. Our moans fill the shower room as elegantly as the steam.

"Baby, if I wasn't struggling to stand and covered in bruises, I'd be starting my forever with you."

"Yes. My Dark Knight, you are my forever. I can wait. It was your eyes that drew me to you and your soul captured mine. I love you. I don't want to spend another moment without you in it."

She rises on her toes, as I come down to her level and our mouths meet in a promise of forever. This is it. The purest start to forever. A kiss that says it all. We still have the vandalism to deal with, yet at this moment there is nothing other than Kate.

We finish up the shower and make our way to her bed. Wrapping my arms around Kate and gluing myself to her body is the new way I want to sleep every night.

Just as I feel myself nodding off to sleep, Kate whispers, "Your eyes used to occupy my dreams. The obsidian-eyed man would come into my dreams and fix all my problems. A hero in the night with eyes as dark as the midnight sky which was his playground."

I squeeze her that little bit tighter so she knows I heard her, understood and will do anything to be her knight. "I promise baby, I'll fix all of this. I'll be your hero. Your Dark Knight."

Lightly kissing her shoulder and resting my head on the pillow next to hers, my eyelids are getting too heavy to keep open. And with a relaxing sigh I hear Kate whisper, "you already are."

It's been two days since Kate came and rescued me. The first day I barely rose from our bed. I told her to go to work, there was nothing she could do, and I just wanted to rest. I was able to get around, so I didn't need her here and I knew she was a little worried about her business.

Leaving this morning, I could tell she was still worried about the vandalism. Although there had been no more attempts, she'd told me they were never regular anyway. She had some details, it wasn't hard evidence and with that being held over our heads, the house at the Belmont Estate still needed to be repaired. I'd seen the pain in her eyes when she'd mentioned the last vandalism on the build. I'd put her at ease with the reassurance that everything would work out in the long run.

I've been able to keep the house for her. Making sure there's a nice meal waiting, no laundry. Domestic things that perhaps most men wouldn't think to do. For Kate, I'd do anything and more.

I know for us to truly have our forever with no black clouds hanging over our head the issue with the vandalism and Noah Fox needs to be addressed.

On our final sweep through my father's house, I

had collected his phone. Plugging it in and beginning to recharge it, I think about how after everything he'd try to take from me, I'd managed to escape it all and find so much more. Even though I've lost my twin and mother, I've gained a life and freedom that neither had ever experienced. Miry was able to find some solace at school. Her friends brought her joy for the small time they were in her presence. Somehow, he'd managed to ensure the truth of how Miry died was kept from the gossip chains and there was nothing I could do being locked in the basement and his lie of me being too distraught to come out after her death. When I was finally released it was with a warning and enough bruises and scars to ensure I kept my mouth shut.

Drowning in the bathtub with weights on her chest was how she'd taken her life. A note hidden in my room had said,

> When they drain the water, they'll release all my pain. I'll be free, twin. I hope one day you will find enough freedom for both of us.
> All my strength, Miry-Bear xx.

The noise of notifications on his phone brings me from memory lane. Making my way over to the kitchen bench where I've hooked up the mobile to charge, I see there are messages from his work asking if he is alright because he hasn't come in. A few women have texted, asking if he needed some 'comfort'. I hadn't realised that a monster like him was needed by so many people. He'd never shown any of those feelings to his family.

There's a message from an unknown number that piques my interest.

UNKNOWN

> Is the job done? I paid you a lot of money to get rid of your son. I expected you to have it done by now.

There's no name, but I know this is Noah Fox. My father had said he was paid to get rid of me, so that Noah could be with Kate.

A message comes through from the unknown number again.

UNKNOWN

> IS IT DONE?

My hands are trembling. He still wants Kate. My Kate. A violent surge rushes through my body. Half my blood is my father's. The monster who inflicted enough pain to drive my mother and twin to an early grave, caused all my injuries and countless other incidents, it's all flowing through my veins at this given moment mixing with the desire to protect Kate. My mother would comfort me and say I would never become him. I will only ever protect the ones I love. And I love Kate. My mother knew I had violence in me, but I never let it out unless it was needed for protection.

I type.

EDWARD

> It's done! Your woman is probably at home crying over that little prick. Go to her.

The ping is within seconds.

UNKNOWN

> You've done this world a service. The next payment will be in your account shortly.

Three things happened within moments of that final message; The money is in the account; I destroy the mobile phone, and a truck is pulling into the driveway.

I can see him saunter up to the house like the long-lost boyfriend with a large bunch of purple hyacinths and daffodils. He doesn't even knock on the front door; he just opens it as I slip into the area behind the kitchen. "Katie. I'm here. Are you alright?"

It was so easy to draw him here. It was like he was just around the corner waiting for the message. Waiting for the moment to pounce and take her back. The fucker doesn't even know Kate. There is no way she would ever take him back.

"Katie, where are you?"

He still doesn't seem worried that she's not answering him. He begins to make his way to the stairs. I can't let him go up there. That's our space. He's already tarnished enough of our place by being in it.

I step out from my hiding space in the wet room. "She's not here."

A look of surprise crosses his face. His calculation of the messages and turn of events can be read across his face. Pure hatred is creeping up his features and every muscle in his body begins to grow taunt.

"You're supposed to be dead."

I walk further into the kitchen, making sure I can see everything this beast has on offer. I can't be sure he's not carrying a weapon. He's built like someone who knows how to fight. Even if he isn't concealing a weapon, he's still just as dangerous.

"And you're not supposed to be here. She doesn't want you, Noah. Leave, and no one has to get hurt. Just leave us alone."

I know my words have no value on this man. I just need to keep him focused on me so I can move further into the kitchen and closer to the knife I've got hiding.

"Flynn, it's you who isn't supposed to be here. I've paid a lot of money to get rid of you and I always get my money's worth."

I get a feeling that keeping him talking will be better for me, and a few things seem to be falling into place. I just have a few questions that need answering. "How did you know who I am? Wait, were you watching us that first night I was here? I saw crushed flowers in the garden bed the next morning."

An evil glint like every villain in the movies crosses his face as he moves to put the bunch of flowers on the table and come closer to me. "And here I was thinking you were some dumb kid. Yes, I was here. I watch my woman more often than she knows. All it took was a call to Rick to find out about you and the rest was supposed to be history. Clearly your deadbeat father couldn't finish a simple task. I guess if you want something done right you should always do it yourself."

I nearly miss the gun being withdrawn from his waistband and having it pointed at my chest.

Bringing a knife to a gunfight—I should've thought this through a little more. I can't wait until the day I no longer have to fight for every breath I need.

Looking around while the gun is aimed at my chest, I see everything I want my life to be. Photos of Kate. Stacks of contracts and orders for builds. The warmth of it all spreads through to my soul. I know she'll miss me, as much as I'll miss her, but I can't let her be with this animal.

Raising my hands above my head and leaving the knife and my phone on the bench, "You win Noah, but don't do it here. If you truly love her, don't leave the blood here for her to clean up." I walk up to him. "Take me away."

The victorious smile stretches across his features. I've already recorded our little interaction, so no matter what, Kate will be protected. It may not have been a deep confession, but it's enough to start an investigation against Noah.

Moving as fast as I can, I smash the gun from his grip and with a well-aimed right hook, I send Noah Fox staggering away from his fallen gun.

With no formal training, I'm running on adrenaline while I wrestle Noah to the ground, hoping to knock him out so I can call the sheriff.

Nevertheless, we are equally matched, and more punches are thrown between us, both wanting the upper hand.

The desire to have a life with Kate keep the punches flying from both of us. Neither of us are prepared to give in. It's now a matter of fighting for our lives.

CHAPTER 11
KATE

Two days feels like an eternity when you've no idea if the vandalism will happen. Or if everyone you meet could be up against you, ready to knock you down and pull the rug out from under your feet. The silver lining is knowing Flynn is safe and at home waiting for me. I've kept my app open to track his phone, just in case. After all, we left Edward unconscious, not dead.

Being back at the Belmont Estate is bittersweet, knowing this is where it all started. Where the eyes of my dreams became a reality. Where my heart reached out and captured another, holding it tight in my ribs, while my head fought the logic in having this man in my life after finding him at the building site.

I had to tell the owners what had happened and the relief when they told me they still wanted me to complete their dream home was nothing short of exhilarating and rewarding. My builds remain what people want because they are made with love, care, honour and integrity. Those little praises helped me realise that there are good people out there wanting quality homes.

The helpers the sheriff had sent over to assist with clean up are all finished. It's back to my team and I to start again. No one is here at the moment because the build was past lock up stage with the painting just started and they had been assigned to other builds. Being here alone gives me the time to focus on the build and my relationship with Flynn. Every minute I'm away from him I want to return to him to tell him again how much I love him. However, this house, like all the others, is my livelihood. I can't just swoon over my man.

I'm upstairs starting on the plastering when I see the sheriff pulling up outside. Hope sparks in my chest that he's here with something positive. I had given him the information that Noah had told me at the cafe after I'd arrived home with Flynn.

Dropping my tools, I head downstairs, meeting the sheriff at the doorway.

"Looking better than the last time." His eyes are showing his age. A few extra grey hairs around his temple, but the banter comment says he's still got a few good years in him yet.

"Me or the house?" The smile on his face means I've said the right thing.

"Both would be the right response to that question. But you look different Miss Kate. Is that apprentice fixing more than houses? I'm not going to lie. I didn't trust him at first with you. But now I see how you look, and I know there's no one else for you."

"John, you've no idea what that means to me. Thank you."

Our smiles are matching. Warm, with respect, admiration and now trust that we've got each other's best interest in mind.

"So why are you here, Sheriff? I'm kind of busy. I can still finish this build within a reasonable time frame depending on a few factors and I don't want to let the clients down. They're still trusting me with their dream home."

He removes his hat and rubs a hand over his head. This is not a friendly gesture. This means business and I'm ready. I want this over with. I want to be able to safely go to bed in my man's arms and arrive at a jobsite without the worry that everything will be demolished when I get there.

"Sorry Kate, the information that you gave me yesterday wasn't a lot to go on, to go after Noah and then Rick. I trust you and I believe you, but money can buy a lot these days including the best way to keep you out of jail. However, we've got the prints back from the last vandalism hit on this house and that is something we can go off. That is solid evidence." His pause is excruciating. Taking in a huge breath he continues,

"We found evidence that links Rick and a few other men to the vandalism. Plus, there is more evidence that supports the accusations against Noah Fox and Rick's involvement. A file has come across my desk with enough information to ensure Noah and Rick never see clear daylight again. They will always have bars or wires in their views"

It's sad that this is where Rick has landed. He was supposed to be my foreman. The man who is able to run my business if anything happens to me on a daily basis. Yet this all feels like he has been here this whole time waiting for the most opportune moment to strip it all back and leave me with nothing. *A file across my desk?* Mac. It must be. I guess that man was worth every orgasm and phone call since, including the message I sent two days ago saying I was safe at home with Flynn. I didn't want him sending the cavalry looking for me.

Taking in a big breath, I ask, "What do we do now?"

"I came out here to ask where Rick Jones is. I need to arrest him on multiple charges. We also need to find Noah Fox. The deputy is out looking for him now."

"I have no idea about Noah Fox. Rick is over at Hillsview Estate doing touch-ups. That's the last place I sent him. I'm coming with you. I have a few questions for him that aren't part of the investigation, they're personal and after you've arrested him, I don't want to see him again."

Nodding, we turn and make our way to our vehicles to go and secure my future without the hassle and pain of the past interrupting it.

When we arrive at Hillsview Estate, Rick's work truck is still there. I can't believe I'm here for this reason. That the one employee who I thought I could trust with everything turns out to be the most devious one on the books.

I follow the sheriff into the house. Happy banter and comments flying around can be heard from the workers. This is what I wanted for my business, like an extension to a family. A work family.

"Rick, I need you to come with me." The sheriff's voice is a directive that no one would argue with. His tone has a caring and understanding tone to it that ensures Rick follows him without question. This is the easiest option and Rick knows it. Placing his roller in the tray, he walks towards the sheriff. Nodding to the other guys there. Looking at my other workers on his team, I really hope no one else is involved in all of this.

Rick reaches the sheriff's side and notices me. It's then that he realises what this is all about and there truly is no way out of it. At the sheriff's vehicle, John gives Rick a pat down then reads him his rights, pulling his arms behind him to secure the handcuffs.

"I only have one question," I say. "Why?"

Rick's smile is one that would put all villains in history to shame. The victory in his eyes. He thinks he's won, that he'll be back here tomorrow.

"I have no family left. Vixen was everything to me. My very reason for breathing. And Noah saw the pain I was going through. You kept growing your business, your life didn't change. Vixen was like a sister to you, but you showed no emotion when my heart and soul was buried that day. She was pregnant, our first child was taken along with her. All I wanted was for you to lose the only thing you seemed to care about, your fucking business. For years, I tried to pull the rug out from under you. But nothing worked until Noah approached me and we discussed the vandalism and kicked it all up a few notches. Then you were starting to hurt and from there I was beginning to feel again."

"I'm truly sorry for your loss. What happened to Vixen shouldn't happen to anyone. But I gave you foreman status, anything you wanted."

Lowering his voice to a deadly whisper he adds, "But I want everything. I was waiting for you to crumble so I could take all of this from you as well."

"You've lost Rick." I stand up to my full height and face him. "I hope you get some help, but you've got nothing from me."

My words are slowly sinking into him as he realises what I've said, and the sheriff lowers him into the backseat. I see there is still a spark of victory there. Adding the final blow before the sheriff closes the door. "And I'd do ten times worse. Include getting rid of that apprentice to have you feel all my pain."

John turns back to me. "You alright Kate?"

"Fuck!" Looking at the sheriff, I see it. He's reading between the lines as well. "I need to know he's safe." I'm beginning to panic again.

I'm running over to my truck as the sheriff is racing around to the driver's side, yelling at me to get home while he calls all officers to my house. I'll need to explain to the workers what's happened with Rick, but Flynn is more important at this point.

I send Flynn a quick message to let him know I'm coming home, but there's no instant reply like what's been happening since he's been home.

The closer I get to my house, the knots start to form in my stomach. This is not what I wanted to feel as I turn into my street. Blue and red lights are flashing from my driveway as I break the speed limit, closing the distance from the top of the street to my address.

Rushing out of my truck I'm confronted with the deputy putting handcuffs on Noah, and Flynn standing in the doorway with a busted face similar to Noah's. Whatever happened at my place has me thinking of even more questions. But the only one I want to ask is directed at Flynn.

Racing pass Noah, I pull up short. "Are you ok? Stupid question. But are you alright?" My brain is so fried at the moment with everything that's happened today and over the last week.

I can't wait any longer, regardless of the audience around us, I jump into his arms and wrapping my legs around his waist, I kiss every part of him I can.

Flynn can't answer my question anyway. He's probably in pain from his father's bruises and whatever happened with Noah. But he's kissing me with just as much passion as what I'm administering to him.

A throat clears behind us, and I turn to see the deputy nervously running his hand through his hair. "Sorry to interrupt, Miss Kate. I was out on patrol thinking about where Noah Fox could be hiding out and it clicked that if he was after you, he was likely close to your place. Making a beeline here, I got here just in time to see him holding Flynn at gun point yelling obscenities at him. The rest isn't important, we have him now. You're safe."

"So, you didn't hear the sheriff sending all patrols here?" Just as I finish several patrol cars roll up lighting up the street with flashing lights and sounds causing a cacophony.

"I guess not. Already got it done. I'll deal with this," He says, nodding to all the officers coming up my driveway.

"Thanks."

Turning on his heels, he heads back to his patrol car, telling everyone to leave, before driving away with all the officers following his orders.

Without putting me down, Flynn walks us into the house and up to our bedroom. He lowers me to standing and starts to remove my clothes. Our kisses are no longer passionate and hungry. They've changed to caring, caressing, love and forever. He is my forever. My life. My heart.

I remove his shirt. Looking deep in his gorgeous black eyes, my fingers leave goosebumps on his abs as I work my way down to the top of his tracksuit pants. Hooking my fingers in the band, I slowly lower his pants and boxer briefs, watching as his hard cock springs free.

Sinking to my knees and kissing my way down his body as I lick along his long shaft, his moan escapes. "You know I won't last long as it is, and I want this to be perfect."

"It will be perfect because it'll be with you." I have plenty of time to take him in my mouth, however, this is all about starting our forever.

Standing, taking in each other, Flynn caresses my face with the back of his knuckles, "I love you, Kate Trembley. I have nothing but you. No money. No training. Just love for you."

Tears begin to fill my eyes, blocking the most handsome and caring man from my view. A silent tear skates down my cheek. He wipes it away with his thumb. Nodding, allowing more tears to fall, I say, "I love you. Forever."

CHAPTER 12
FLYNN

Every minute of every day for the rest of my life I'll be grateful and thankful for this beautiful woman.

Kissing her deeply, I start unbuttoning her work shirt. I've never been more thankful to have a full button-down work shirt as I am right now. Making quick work of all her clothes, we're standing completely naked and wanting in front of each other.

Pulling back from another scorching kissing session, I cup her face and gaze deep into her crystal pools. All that can be seen is a promise of forever, no matter what.

"I love you" is whispered from both of us as we cover each other's faces with soft kisses. I slide my hands under her thighs and lift her up. Her wet core is resting against my hard cock. Moaning with even the lightest touch, my blood is full of electricity as it travels around my body and gathering everything to move south to my throbbing cock. Her legs wrap around my body, locking her ankles around my waist, like she doesn't want to let me go. I'm not letting her go either.

Her moans keep escaping along with her pants. I haven't fully healed from my beatings, including the few Noah got in, but there's nothing that will keep me from her tonight— or any night.

Lowering her down to the bed, I leave her mouth, making tracks with my lips and tongue all the way down her curvy, soft, workers body, stopping at the apex of her thighs.

Pushing her legs further open, I lightly start blowing on her clit. She's so responsive the lightest touch sends her back arching off the mattress. If I don't give her an orgasm soon, I won't even make it into her pussy. She's so gorgeous. I lick from her centre, opening her folds and flicking her clit at the end. Her hand dives into my hair holding me in place while she grinds herself on my tongue. Using me for her own pleasure.

"Fuck. I'm close."

My fingers enter her with no resistance due to the juices flowing from her soaking pussy. A few pumps and Kate is screaming my name, panting and moaning, trying to catch her breath.

Softly licking her through her orgasm, she pulls me up her body, wanting to taste the arousal and take it from my tongue. Sucking on my tongue, she moans with delight at the sweet taste of herself.

Kate releases one of her hands and reaches between us to grab my cock. It's hard, throbbing and there's no way I can make this last or be great for her. I know she's mine, but she's been with others. She's more experienced than me. I'm not sure if my love is enough for her to be satisfied with my performance.

Sensing my trepidation in making this perfect for her, she places my cock at her entrance. "Stop overthinking this and fuck me. I want you. Only you. Forever you."

She's so wet from her orgasm and her walls are contracting around my cock. With one thrust I'm all the way into the hilt and I don't want to move. Fuck, she's so tight. Any movement and I'll blow.

"Fuck you feel so good." She's clenching my cock. Running her nails over my back, sending goosebumps covering every surface. "Fuck me, until you come." Her breathy pants are giving me all the encouragement I need.

Knowing I won't last, I'm focused on her eyes, trying not to shoot my load in less than five pumps. "Baby, it won't take long."

"Then we'll do it again and again. I know the boss, I'm sure I can get the day off tomorrow to spend it in bed with you."

Slowly moving back out of her until my crown is just resting at her entrance, it feels amazing. Even more so when I push back inside her and grind my base right along her clit. There is no better place than right here with Kate, the woman I love.

The pleasure is building at the base of my spine. I can't hold back anymore. Increasing the pace, I'm lost in the pure desire and fully encompassing feeling of this beautiful woman. Burying deep in her pussy, I come and shoot my load deep in my woman. Stream after hot sticky stream just keep coming out filling her up.

Resting my head in the crook of her neck and shoulders, I probably shouldn't have the urge to go again but Kate's gentle, encouraging kisses have me working myself back up again, while keeping my cock buried deep within her pussy.

Rolling over and wrapping Kate in my arms, I notice it's not long after midnight. We've explored each other's body and a loud grumble comes from Kate's belly.

"I think that's a sign we need to stop and replenish." I say, kissing the back of her neck and shoulders. I can't get enough of her.

"I think you're right. Come on, I'll make us some French toast." She replies, climbing off the bed

Normally I'd protest her doing anything after a long day on the tools and I know that she had to deal with the arrest of Rick as well. But hours of making love and exploring each other's body would have anyone starving.

Crawling out of bed, we grab lounge clothes and head down to the kitchen. Never more than an arm's length away from each other, the atmosphere is calm and reassuring.

Waiting for the French toast to cook, I stand with Kate wrapped in my arms. Flipping the egg and bread mixture, she leans further into my shoulders.

The comfortable silence of knowing that we have forever stretches around us mixing with the sweet cinnamon scents of the French toast. A thought rushes through my mind.

"How soon can we get married?"

With a little giggle and a shake of her head, Kate turns the frying pan off and turns to wrap her arms around my neck. "I reckon I can pull some strings with the sheriff and get it done soon. Although that wasn't much of a proposal."

Drawing her in for a kiss, I nod against her lips. "You know it's forever baby, just thought a piece of paper would make it official. Now let's eat this French toast so I can go back and eat you for dessert."

"Yes, sir."

EPILOGUE
KATE

Five Years Later

Sitting in a meeting listening to Flynn explain his plans with Marcus for the restoration project has every fibre in my body igniting with passion for my husband.

A lot has changed in the past five years. I held my promise to Flynn and the sheriff married us as soon as legally possible. Drew and his partner Brad were our witnesses and John officiated the ceremony. It was perfect. It was only after our blissful happy day that a parcel came in the mail. Mac had sent us a photo of Flynn and I gazing into each other's eyes at such a beautiful angle. His message written in his terrible handwriting, *'I've always got you. He's a good one.'* Flynn had freaked out a little. I had to call and confront him about how the fuck he'd known about our wedding.

"Stalker much? What the fuck Mac, how did you know about my wedding?"

He chuckled like he thought he'd really done nothing wrong. "I've still got access to your phone. I like Flynn, he's good for you."

Still fuming, but with the flames slowly dying at anyone praising my husband, I quickly add, "You'll un-hack my phone or whatever you do, if you know what's good for you."

"Alright darling, just for you." He was still laughing at me as I hung up on him.

When Flynn finally met Mac and Logan, there was no animosity over the wedding picture stunt and was enlarged and hangs on our living room wall. They have tried to encourage Flynn to the gaming world. But everyone agreed that a tradie's life is where Flynn's true skills lie.

Drew became foreman after the issues with Rick, and I had to tell the painters what had happened with him, after we found out that no one else from Make-It-Able had been involved with the vandalism.

Rick unfortunately died in a prison incident. Although no one deserves that ending, when Sheriff John told us, we stopped looking over our shoulders wondering if he'd re-emerge from the short sentence he was serving. He'd managed to buy a reduced sentence somehow, with the money from Vixen's estate. Noah is still locked deep in the state penitentiary that houses the worst of the worst. His final days will be seen through bars and wires.

The sheriff had come knocking a week after the incident with Rick and Noah asking about Flynn's father. We were able to honestly fill him in on the situation, with Flynn opening up to what horrors he had faced in his life. However, we were no help to the investigation surrounding the mysterious house fire and Edward Davies slumped in a chair in the loungeroom dead.

"Alright, Marcus, that's about it. I can start to restore your designer printing shop up the coast Monday. It will take around six months. Just bear in mind, timing isn't exact in the trade industry." Flynn shakes our new client's hand, showing even more personal growth than the quiet, dark-eyed young man caught in my build all those years ago.

My Dark Knight continues to be the hero in my life. It was on a small vacation to an original village in the state with heritage buildings that Flynn's love for restoration was sparked. That night while lying in bed wrapped in each other's arms in a post-sex haze, Flynn announced, "I don't want children, and I want to learn and add restoration to your company."

He never could add 'our' to Make-It-Able, even though I asked him too constantly. He even took my surname in our wedding ceremony. Flynn wanted complete freedom from his past. "I'm sorry if you want kids, but I can't bring them into this world. My father tarnished my love for little people. But I want to help others like me."

I fell more in love with my husband in the little village in a colonial house. From then on Flynn had studied restoration techniques and added it to Make-It-Able. And together we continue to work with organisations to assist with children from abusive households.

Watching Marcus leave, I turn back to Flynn standing at the head of the meeting table in the office. When his dark eyes lock with my crystal ones, I know there's only one outcome. Moving together, driven by an insatiable lust we lock lips with hands roaming over each other's body.

Pulling apart to gaze in my eyes, Flynn asks, "Do you think we're safe from Drew's shitty timing?"

Giggling while I'm undoing Flynn's belt and work pants, memories of Drew nearly catching us in a post coitus state at building sites has been a little awkward. Drew, ever the comedian, took it in his stride.

Pulling Flynn's velvet, hard cock from his trousers, using pre-cum to rub him from base to tip, listening to his pleasurable moan, I say, "Drew isn't working today. We should be safe. Now how are you going to fuck me, Dark Knight?"

He reaches for the hem of my shirt, ripping it over my head. His lips are covering mine with his, as his hands push the cups of my bra below my breasts, spilling the heavy globes out into his hands. Massaging them and tweaking my nipples, Flynn pulls back only far enough to whisper across my lips. "I'm going to lay you across this table and watch these glorious tits bounce while I thrust every hard inch in and out of you. Any issues with that, take it up with the boss."

My moan is echoed around the office space as I picture everything he's describing. I can feel the moisture pooling in the bottom of my panties. My quiet, shy, virgin no longer exists. It's all hot passion and desire that flows between us now.

Before I know it, I'm lying on my back across the conference table with my husband gazing over my worker's curves with complete devotion and passion in his stare. I'm so wet that Flynn lines himself up and pushes through my soaking channel allowing me to feel every glorious inch. Pressing the base of his throbbing cock against my clit, my orgasm is barrelling to the forefront. He's learnt all the tricks to my body but surprises me every time.

"Put your arms above your head and don't fucking move them."

The dominating bedroom demands from Flynn make my orgasm rise too fast, but last and return repeatedly.

Thrust after passionate thrust, Flynn makes my tits bounce, just like he promised. It doesn't take long before we're both panting and screaming our combined release around the office.

Holding himself above me on his elbows. Our bodies covered in a light sheen of sweat, Flynn kisses me with complete tenderness. The opposite to the animalistic approach he just demonstrated. Whispering over my lips with the words broken by his kisses. "I love you, Mrs. Kate Trembley. My light. My life."

Capturing his face with my hands on either side of his face. "I love you, Mr. Flynn Trembley. My Dark Knight. My saviour."

Our combined confessions have him growing hard inside me again. It seems round two is in order and I'll need to clean the office before Drew and the others come in for a staff meeting tomorrow.

ACKNOWLEDGMENTS

Firstly, you the reader. If you've picked this up and are sticking with me, I truly appreciate the time it's taken you to get to this part of the book. Thank you for taking a chance on me. And know there is more to come.

My friends, mates, people and family. Your support with my emotions, messages and random outbursts of expression are the reasons I can continue doing what I love. No matter our distance or time apart I've felt the love and gratitude and wouldn't be able to continue this journey without you.

Thanks to my team as I think you can be called. My cover designer, Tash. I love our rugby chats and ability to swap between work and rugby so seamlessly. My editor, Steph. Glad we kept some darkness. Kate and Flynn needed to be told this way. My agent, Katherine. Thank you for setting up my Tess life and dealing with all the behind-the-scenes stuff so I can just write.

For everyone reading this, stay tuned for more, we're not done.

Love fiercely,

Tess xxoo

ABOUT THE AUTHOR

Tess Molesworth grew up in a small country town in NSW, and now lives not far from there.

A lover of life, writing and spending time with close friends, Tess' superpower is her infectious laughter that leaves you wanting more.

Tess is a compassionate and ardent dreamer who is always willing to tell you a story, and can be found crafting them in her favourite local pub.

ALSO BY TESS MOLESWORTH

BOOK ONE - The Assistant

https://tessmolesworth.com/shop/p/the-assistant-by-tess-molesworth

BOOK TWO - The Apprentice

https://tessmolesworth.com/shop/p/the-assistant-by-tess-molesworth-2btzd

<u>Coming Soon (2025)</u>

BOOK THREE - The Hacker

BOOK FOUR - The Designer

www.ingramcontent.com/pod-product-compliance
Lightning Source LLC
LaVergne TN
LVHW091555060526
838200LV00036B/841